"It's not enough just to be your first, Cass."

Paul took a deep breath, ignored the thickening of his voice and made himself go on. "Honey, you're the kind of woman who needs and deserves everything a man has to give—his name, his children, his forever after. That's not me. I wish it was, but it's not. Somewhere out there is a man who'll be your one and only, and I won't rob you of that just to be your first, not even if it kills me."

"Why does it have to be like this?" she asked.

He steeled himself and said, "Because I messed up, honey. Now, let me go before this attack of decency passes."

"Paul, please stay."

But they both knew he couldn't. He looked down at her one last time. "Goodbye, Cass. And thank you."

At that moment Paul knew for once he'd done the right thing for someone else at his own expense, and that someone was Cassidy. No one mattered more....

Dear Reader,

You'll find the heartwarming themes of love and family in our November Romance novels. First up, longtime reader favorite Arlene James portrays *A Bride To Honor.* In this VIRGIN BRIDES title, a pretty party planner falls for a charming tycoon...whom another woman seeks to rope into a loveless marriage! But can honorable love prevail?

A little tyke takes a tumble, then awakes to ask a rough-hewn rancher, *Are You My Daddy?* So starts Leanna Wilson's poignant, emotional romance between a mom and a FABULOUS FATHER who "pretends" he's family. Karen Rose Smith finishes her enticing series DO YOU TAKE THIS STRANGER? with *Promises, Pumpkins and Prince Charming.* A wealthy bachelor lets a gun-shy single mom believe he's just a regular guy. Will their fairy-tale romance survive the truth?

FOLLOW THAT BABY, Silhouette's exciting cross-line continuity series, comes to Romance this month with *The Daddy and the Baby Doctor* by star author Kristin Morgan. An ex-soldier single dad butts heads with a beautiful pediatrician over a missing patient. Temperatures rise, pulses race—could marriage be the cure? It's said that opposites attract, and when *The Cowboy and he Debutante* cozy up on a rustic ranch...well, you'll just have to read this TWINS ON THE DOORSTEP title by Stella Bagwell to find out! A hairdresser dreams of becoming a *Lone Star Bride* when a handsome stranger passes through town. Don't miss the finale of Linda Varner's THREE WEDDINGS AND A FAMILY miniseries!

Beloved authors Lindsay Longford, Sandra Steffen, Susan Meier and Carolyn Zane return to our lineup next month, and in the new year we launch our brand-new promotion, FAMILY MATTERS. So keep coming back to Romance!

Happy Thanksgiving!

Mary-Theresa Hussey
Senior Editor, Silhouette Romance

Please address questions and book requests to:
Silhouette Reader Service
U.S.: 3010 Walden Ave., P.O. Box 1325, Buffalo, NY 14269
Canadian: P.O. Box 609, Fort Erie, Ont. L2A 5X3

VIRGIN BRIDES
A BRIDE TO HONOR

Arlene James

Silhouette
ROMANCE™
Published by Silhouette Books
America's Publisher of Contemporary Romance

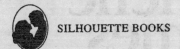

SILHOUETTE BOOKS

ISBN 0-373-19330-0

A BRIDE TO HONOR

Copyright © 1998 by Deborah A. Rather

This edition published by arrangement with Harlequin Books S.A.

® and TM are trademarks of Harlequin Books S.A., used under license. Trademarks indicated with ® are registered in the United States Patent and Trademark Office, the Canadian Trade Marks Office and in other countries.

Printed in U.S.A.

Books by Arlene James

Silhouette Romance

City Girl #141
No Easy Conquest #235
Two of a Kind #253
A Meeting of Hearts #327
An Obvious Virtue #384
Now or Never #404
Reason Enough #421
The Right Moves #446
Strange Bedfellows #471
The Private Garden #495
The Boy Next Door #518
Under a Desert Sky #559
A Delicate Balance #578
The Discerning Heart #614
Dream of a Lifetime #661
Finally Home #687
A Perfect Gentleman #705
Family Man #728
A Man of His Word #770
Tough Guy #806
Gold Digger #830
Palace City Prince #866
*The Perfect Wedding #962
*An Old-Fashioned Love #968
*A Wife Worth Waiting For #974
Mail-Order Brood #1024
*The Rogue Who Came To Stay #1061
*Most Wanted Dad #1144
Desperately Seeking Daddy #1186
*Falling for a Father of Four #1295
A Bride To Honor # 1330

Silhouette Special Edition

A Rumor of Love #664
Husband in the Making #776
With Baby in Mind #869
Child of Her Heart #964
*The Knight, the Waitress
  and the Toddler* #1131
Every Cowgirl's Dream #1195

Silhouette Books

Fortune's Children

Single with Children

*This Side of Heaven

ARLENE JAMES

grew up in Oklahoma and has lived all over the South. In 1976 she married "the most romantic man in the world." The author enjoys traveling with her husband, but writing has always been her chief pastime.

Dear Reader,

I knew I was going to like Cassidy Jane Penno, the heroine of *A Bride To Honor,* from the moment she popped into my mind. Cassidy is pragmatic but charmingly quirky. She is a woman of firm conviction and unconditional love. What's not to like?

Frankly, I wasn't so sure about Paul Barclay Spencer. After all, Paul lets himself get into a tricky situation. But Paul turned out to be the finest of men, one who recognizes real treasure, who properly appreciates the rare and the true, a modern man of genuine honor. For Paul, like Cassidy, love runs much deeper than its physical expression, though even *he* didn't understand that about himself until it was almost too late.

It is that very principle that stands at the heart of the VIRGIN BRIDES series. We romantics know that true romance is about the depth of reward to be found in the expression of true love, physically and otherwise. Without love, sex is empty and totally self-serving. Within the context of total love and heartfelt commitment, sex is one of God's greatest gifts to humankind. Cassidy's innate wisdom tells her this from early on. It's a truth that Paul has to learn the hard way, but learn it he does, and his reward is *A Bride To Honor.*

God bless all true romantics,

Arlene James

Chapter One

"I know it's important," Cassidy said, righting her red yarn wig and dusting off her white, ruffled pinafore. "It's just that it's so close to Halloween, and you know this is the busiest time of the year for me."

William looked as though he wanted to pull his short, expensively styled, yellow blond hair. He took a deep breath, though, and merely straightened his gray silk tie, saying carefully, "That's why I need this favor."

Cassidy smiled and took pity on her too-serious brother. "I said I'd outfit him. I just hope he doesn't want anything too exotic, that's all."

William leaned across the glass display case, ignoring outrageous false eyelashes, rubber noses, skull caps and an impressive assortment of warts and moles, to seize his sister by the front of her Raggedy Ann costume. "I don't think I'm getting through the wig. This is my boss, Cass! He's desperate. I have personally recommended you. For pity's sake, don't let me down!"

Poor William, always in such turmoil, so fearful of being

embarrassed by his family. All right, they were a tad...eccentric. But they meant well. Usually. She laid a mittened hand against his cheek and smiled reassuringly, completely forgetting that her own face was heavily painted with drawn-on eyelashes, red circle cheeks and a Cupid's bow mouth. "I promise, brother dear, Mr. Paul Barclay Spencer of Barclay Bakeries will receive star treatment from me. And we'll find him a costume that will impress this Betty person and make him feel comfortable at the same time. Upon my honor as your sister."

William was only slightly mollified. "It's *Betina*," he said pointedly, "Betina Lincoln, though if all goes well she will almost certainly be *Mrs.* Paul Spencer by spring."

"And Mr. Spencer will have the family business safely back in family hands again," Cassidy said to prove that she had been paying attention after all, "and he'll owe it all to you." She patted William's cheek encouragingly. He caught her hand and pushed it down to her side.

"Yes, if you don't mess up everything. Now will you please, for heaven's sake, get out of that absurd costume before he gets here?"

Cassidy sighed and reached up to tug off her enormous, red yarn wig with one mittened hand while sketching a cross over her heart with the other. "I'll abandon Raggedy Ann for my own mousy persona *and* I'll come up with the perfect costume for your boss, I swear, something that will win him the heart— and the company shares—of the glamorous, elusive Miss Betina Lincoln. Satisfied?"

William straightened, smoothed his unwrinkled Italian suit and nodded tersely. "Just remember, I'm counting on you."

She smiled encouragingly, and he gave her his patented, big brother look of near approval. Then on his way out he ruined it by raking his clear green gaze over her costume-clad self and shaking his head as if to ask how such a promising young executive as himself had wound up being the sibling of such a pitiful goon as her. She honestly didn't know what the problem was. She was a costumer. Costumers by definition designed, sewed and—if they were lucky enough to own their own shops, as she did—stored, displayed, rented, sold and, of course, *wore* costumes. Who on earth would wear a costumer's costume if she didn't wear one herself? Poor uptight William just didn't always see the correlations in life—except as they pertained to him. Still, she reminded herself, the Penno family was a cross for poor William to bear, and she did not want to add to his burden.

He didn't understand the divorce their parents had gone through last year, even though it was obvious to Cassidy that, despite thirty-five years of marriage—or perhaps because of it—Alvin and Anna Penno were completely incompatible. He didn't see that they were both happier on their own or that the failed marriage had nothing whatsoever to do with him or her. She supposed that his association with the Barclay Spencer clan was part of the problem.

That family more than any other of whom she was aware made family and family concerns supreme, especially when it came to the family business, Barclay Bakeries. What must it be like, she wondered, to be part of such a cohesive unit? She supposed it was wonderful, since William seemed to admire and envy them so.

It certainly seemed fitting that Paul Spencer, CEO and general manager of the family bakeries, should marry his stepcousin, especially since she had inherited shares of the company from the late Mr. Chester Barclay, Paul's grandfather. A marriage between the two of them would tie everything up all neat and clean. She couldn't help wondering, though, why "the lovely and sophisticated Miss Lincoln," as described by William, was so reluctant to marry Paul now, especially considering that he had broken off a torrid affair with the woman against her will some months ago. It looked to Cassidy as if *Betina* would be getting everything she wanted with this marriage. But then, perhaps she had misunderstood that portion of her brother's explanation.

Putting the Barclay bunch out of her mind, she started for the changing room, calling Tony away from the new Arabian Nights display that he was putting together out front. He stuck his head into the circus arena that now defined the second of four showrooms in the shop and waggled an eyebrow at her.

"You called, *chérie?*" he asked in an affected French accent. A jaunty straw boater was pushed onto the back of his head, revealing the black widow's peak of which he was so proud. He was Maurice Chevalier today. Yesterday he'd been Clark Gable. Tomorrow, he was sure, he'd be the next great superstar of screen and stage, just as soon as he graduated college and left Dallas behind for Los Angeles or New York. He wasn't quite certain yet which coast he was going to allow to discover him.

At twenty-five, her own dreams of acting success reshaped into a satisfying career as a costumer, Cassidy felt decades older and wiser than her twenty-year-old clerk/assistant Tony Abatto. She could even admit to a bit of impatience with his posturing and half-teasing passes, while at the same time chastising herself for raining, ever so lightly, on his parade. Let him believe in all-consuming passions and shooting-star careers while he could. He'd find out soon enough that it took more than mere talent to get a break in the business. Meanwhile work awaited, and promises had to be kept.

"I'm going to change," she told him. "Watch the shop. I'm expecting a special customer."

"*Oui, mademoiselle.* With my life I shall guard the repository of your dreams, another dedicated expression of the *amour* I bear you."

"Better an expression of the *amour* you bear your job," she said through a stage smile, winding her way through the circus paraphernalia strewn about the floor.

"Raggedy Ann not suit the mood?" Tony asked, coming fully into the room.

"My brother's mood," she tossed over her shoulder, catching the grimace he meant for her back. Tony was of the opinion that William was a Philistine of the grossest order, and while she agreed with him on one level, she felt duty-bound to defend her brother on another. She settled, this time, for a cutting glance, unaware that painted-on eyelashes and bright red grease paint somewhat ruined the effect. "Start a rack for me, Tony," she called, slipping into the curtained alcove.

"Okay. What do you want on it?"

"Oh, the usual macho male themes."

"One Dracula/Fighter Pilot/Corsair coming up."

Cassidy sighed wistfully. She had a Peter Pumpkin Eater costume she'd like to palm off on somebody before Halloween, but she supposed it would not be wise to attempt it with William's boss. On the other hand, every Dracula, pirate and military uniform in the building was reserved. Whatever Paul Spencer chose was bound to send her back to her sewing machine, and just when she'd thought she was through with the season rush. Oh, well, she could sleep the second week of November—if she lasted that long.

Cassidy first pulled off her mitts, then slipped out of the dress with its attached pinafore, hung it on a hook and divested herself of the calf-length bloomers, striped stockings and soft black shoes. Comfortable, snug-fitting jeans and a mustard yellow cardigan sweater worn buttoned to the top of the V-neck replaced the dress and pinafore. Heavy, plain white cotton socks and burgundy penny loafers, complete with the pennies, replaced the stripes and black shoes. Leaving her goldish brown hair pulled back with the aid of a rubber band, she took the costume and left the dressing room. From sheer habit she went directly to the permanent rack where the Raggedy Anns were kept and hung the costume in its proper place before heading to the mirrored makeup station in the far back of the shop.

She loved every inch of her store, but the makeup station was especially dear to her heart owing to the fact that it contained numerous components of her late grandfather's barbershop, from the pole to a lather brush, which she used for dusting on powder. Seating herself in the creaky, green leather chair, she whipped a short cape from a drawer and swirled it around her throat and shoulders before reaching for a tub of cold cream. With her fingertips, she began working the white, red and black grease paint from her face. She had it converted nicely to a gooey, slimy, gray mass ready to be toweled off when a movement in the mirror alerted her that "Maurice" had walked up behind her. Before she could ask why he wasn't watching the front door as he'd been told, he depressed the foot pedal that released the back of the chair and she found herself prone, looking up at her irritating clerk and the front of a dark, pin-striped suit.

"Ewww," Tony said helpfully. Then he bent over and kissed her on the neck, saying huskily in his phony French accent, "This client asked to see you, *chérie.*"

Cassidy took a swing at him with her towel, but he danced back out of reach, laughing, and informed the other man, "She adores me."

"So it would seem," was the acerbic reply.

Groaning, Cassidy dropped the towel over her face. A moment later, the back of her chair shot forward, nearly propelling her out of it, and she heard the rush of expelled air as someone took a seat on the leather upholstered rolling stool at her side. Expecting Tony, she snatched the towel off her head, only to encounter the grinning visage of a stranger. He was a handsome stranger, at least, with short, conservatively styled dark brown hair the color of cocoa powder and sparkling blue-gray eyes framed with thick, reddish brown lashes. His straight, slender brows seemed almost black, as did the hint of beard shadow that seemed to lurk beneath his pale golden skin. The breadth of his smile made hard little apples of his cheeks and cut deep brackets between them and the flat of a rather prominent chin.

He offered her a long, slender hand. "Cassidy Penno, I presume."

She slipped her hand into his mechanically. "Yes."

"Paul Spencer."

She closed her eyes, grimaced and snatched her hand back, using it to mop up the nasty gray grease covering her face. "I'm sorry, Mr. Spencer," she said plaintively from behind the towel, her voice muffled accordingly. "I was dressed as Raggedy Ann earlier, and my brother told me you were coming, but I thought I'd have time to remove my makeup, and that rascal Tony probably wanted to embarrass me, blast him! He hates William, and he stays mad at me because I won't take his passes seriously, and I ought to fire him, I know, but—"

Paul Spencer pulled the towel out of her hands, still grinning. "Uh-huh," he said, wiping gunk from her face in long, sure strokes. Cassidy stared, mesmerized by the sparkle in his eyes. "You were telling me why you weren't going to fire, ah, Tony, was it?"

Cassidy mumbled weakly, "It takes a certain kind of individual to work in a place like this."

"Really?" he said, using the towel to wipe a glob of grease from beneath her eyebrow. "What kind of individual is that?"

She took the towel from his hands and turned to the mirror, leaning forward in order to avoid his gaze as much as to see her own face. Clumps of gray gunk clung to her skin. Quickly she began wiping them away.

"You were telling me what sort of individual works in a place like this," he reminded her, folding his arms.

"Someone who loves the theater," she said tersely. "An actor usually. Someone who likes to dress up. Someone cre-

ative. Someone who'll work for minimum wage." A glance
into the side mirror showed that he was grinning again. She
rubbed furiously at her cheeks, hoping to disguise the color
burning there. William would kill her if he found out about
this! Poor William, forever foiled by his own family. Cassidy
threw down the towel in disgust and ripped the rubber band
from her hair, allowing it to swing about her shoulders in one
sleek sheet as she plucked thin tendrils of bangs forward onto
her forehead. "I'd appreciate it, Mr. Spencer if you wouldn't
tell William that you caught me like this. William's a wonderful brother but he's. . . well, he's—"

"Uptight," Paul Spencer provided helpfully. "Humorless.
Staid."

Cassidy gaped, horrified, at his reflection in the mirror.

Spencer laughed. "Relax, Miss Penno, I think very highly
of your brother. He's a fine executive and an upstanding member of society. He also takes himself and life in general a bit
too seriously." He used his thumb and forefinger to make a
zipping motion across his mouth and added, "William won't
hear a word from me about how you greeted me looking like
some kind of swamp monster."

Cassidy spun the chair around. "I did not!"

"No, you didn't," he agreed, lips quirking. "I was teasing."

"Oh."

The smile working its way across his lips widened to expose
strong, white teeth. One on the right side had a tiny chip in
it. Suddenly, something of his humor infected her, and she
knew, not only that she could trust him, but that he trusted
her enough to joke with her. Why did she sense that there
were precious few others with whom he could laugh? It didn't
really matter. What mattered was that it was going to be all
right. Her spirits soared, and she laughed.

"I'm so sorry. I must have looked a fright."

He chuckled. "Let's just say that I'd never have guessed there was such a pretty face beneath all that gray slime."

She felt a flash of pleasure, then realized that he was teasing again. "Oh, you," she said, getting to her feet and waving him to his. "Actually, in my business it's very convenient to have such a plain, featureless face. It's like having a clean canvas with which to work. If you'll just come this way, I think—I hope—Tony has put together some possibilities for us." To her surprise, he hauled her up short with a hand clamped down on her forearm. Heat flashed up her arm to lodge somewhere in her chest, spreading warmth subtly.

"Who told you that you were plain?" he demanded, brows furrowed. "William?"

"What? Oh…no, of course not!"

"Yours is a very delicate, classical beauty," he insisted, skimming a finger over her wispy brows, down the short—too short, in her opinion—bridge of her nose, across the subtle peaks of her upper lip and over the rounded tip of her chin.

Cassidy was hypnotized. No one had ever told her that she was beautiful before. She almost believed him, he was so good at it! Then he took his finger away, and reality snapped back into place.

She shook her head to clear it and pointed tentatively into the other room. "Shall we?"

He stepped back, dropped his gaze and lifted a hand to indicate that he would follow her. She turned and strode purposefully into the other room, trying not to think how tall he was, not as tall as she had first imagined, because when they had stood close, she had noticed that the top of her head came about to his eyebrows. That meant that he probably wasn't much taller than six feet, as she stood just about five-nine in these shoes. A perverse little gremlin in the back of her mind whispered that he was just about the perfect height for her, when she knew perfectly well that there was no such thing.

To her relief, the rolling rack that they used for the "possibilities'' that customers had not yet tried on, stood in the middle of the third showroom. Cassidy hoped that Tony had used better judgment in choosing costumes than he had used in bringing Paul Spencer back to the makeup station while she was covered in gray glop. She indicated a small barrel, atop which a deep red cushion had been placed. "If you'll just have a seat, Mr. Spencer, I'll show you some of our more popular styles for men."

"Paul," he said, lowering himself onto the cushion.

Not a good idea, she told herself. He was simply too attractive a man to call by his given name, under the circumstances. She merely smiled and reached for the first hanger on the rack, displaying it for him with a flourish.

"This is our most popular costume at this time of year, for obvious reasons."

Paul lifted a neat brow. "Dracula seems a bit trite to me."

"Right." Cassidy moved the costume to the back of the rack and reached for the next one. "The corsair, or pirate, cuts a dashing figure, and it comes complete with earring, saber, and—if you like—peg leg or parrot."

His lips quirked. "I don't think so. I'm not the earring type."

"Okay." To the back of the rack went the corsair, and out came the Red Baron. "This is a very romantic figure, the famous World War I fighter pilot. They have those commercials on television, you know, where the women swoon—"

He was shaking his head. "Swooning women embarrass me."

"Ah." She stowed the Red Baron. "How about Patton? We could silver your hair and pad your middle a bit and have you looking just like George C. Scott."

"I don't think so."

"Dwight D. Eisenhower?"

"I'm not sure the military thing is for me."

"Not even the Rebel soldier from the Civil War?"

He lifted both hands helplessly. "Especially not the Rebel soldier. We're trying to expand beyond the Southern states at Barclay Bakeries, and there will be prospective clients at this party."

"Politically incorrect, huh?"

"I wouldn't want to chance it."

"I guess the Yankee Blue is out of the question, too, then."

"And the American Indian, I'm afraid."

"Hmm." She squinted at his very dark hair and reached for an idea. "I suppose we could try a Chinese emperor. A little makeup around the eyes and a pigtail…"

He merely folded his hands together, clearly underwhelmed.

"Rudolph Valentino as the sheikh?"

He considered that, then shook his head. "Not for this occasion." He looked around him. "And no gypsies."

"Prince Albert?"

"Wasn't he bald?"

"Castro. No forget that."

"And nix on Joseph Stalin just in case he's your next inspiration."

She made a face at him and was rewarded with that quick grin. "Stalin," she murmured. "Russia. Hmm. Oh, my gosh," she said, snapping her fingers. "Remember Tony Curtis in that marvelous old movie about the cossacks? Yul Brynner played his father, I think, and they jumped their horses over wider and wider gorges in a test of bravery."

"*Taras Bulba!*" he said, coming to his feet. "Didn't he die at the end?"

She shrugged. "He still got the girl."

"Oh, yeah." He folded his arms, one finger tapping his chin. "Yeah. I think I can do that." The idea seemed to grow on him, and he nodded enthusiastically. "Well, let's see it."

Oops. Cassidy grimaced apologetically. "Uh, I don't exactly have one in stock, but I can make one up for you."

He stroked his chin. "I suppose it would be an original, just for me."

Cassidy relaxed and smiled, even though it meant research for which she didn't have time, not to mention designing, cutting and sewing—and fittings. She reminded herself that this was for William and said resignedly, "Exactly."

"Excellent!" He rubbed his hands together enthusiastically. "So, how do we begin?"

"With research, actually."

"Research! Very good. Where should I begin? I mean, what era historically?"

She blinked at him. "You don't have to do the research yourself. That's my job."

"Well, how will I know you're doing it correctly?" he asked.

She chewed the inside of her cheek. "Good point."

He laughed. "It's not that I don't trust you. I'm just something of a purist, I guess. Anyway, I like to *know* things, and I don't want to look like an idiot if someone asks me about my costume."

"Very well," she said, oddly touched. "You might want to research the movie, too, then. In fact, it's more likely you'll be asked about that than the historical significance of the costume."

He considered this, nodding. "I see your point. It's a pity that people always seem to be more interested in the movie than the history. I think we diminish ourselves with our lack of interest in history."

"You know, I hadn't thought that," she said, impressed.

He seemed oddly pleased. "Ah. Well. I, um, guess I'm off to do some research. Uh, what comes after that?"

"Oh!" Cassidy realized she hadn't thought about fitting appointments. "We'll have to have fittings, of course."

"But, um, isn't there something before that? I mean, I will

get a chance to approve the overall design beforehand, won't I? Or is that too—"

"No! No, it's fine. Really. In fact, it'll probably save time... really."

He smiled at her. "Fine. So, um, when do I get to see the designs?"

Oh, jeepers, she had so much to do, deliveries to make, pickups at the dry cleaners, various mending, several alterations. She tried to think, then heard herself saying, "End of the week?"

"How about Thursday?" he suggested. "Friday's pretty sewed up for me."

Sewed up was an apt description for Cassidy's whole week, but she shrugged, anyway. "Thursday, then. How about late in the day, say, after five?"

He put a finger to one temple, thinking. "I wouldn't want to keep you late. When do you take lunch?"

"I beg your pardon?" Lunch? What was that?

"Before or after good old Tony?"

"Er, after."

"About one, then?"

She tried to reason out why this was not a good idea, but all she could think was that Tony had morning classes on Thursday. He wouldn't want to, but he could come in by one. She nodded dumbly.

"Great. Shall we go out, or it would be better if I brought something in?"

He was going to feed her? "Oh, you don't need to—"

"Nonsense. I have to eat even if you don't, and frankly, a good meal wouldn't hurt you any. Not that you're too thin! Heavens, no! I just meant..." His gaze traveled over her tall, slender form appreciatively. "Well," he said, absently straightening his tie, "you obviously don't have a problem with your weight. In fact, I'd bet you're one of those naturally slender females other women just hate."

Her mouth was hanging open. She couldn't help it. Unless she'd lost her mind, which was a distinct possibility, he was actually flirting with her. Her! Cassidy Jane Penno. "Uh, yab, duh, er…"

He just laughed and chucked her under the chin, then abruptly checked his watch. "Gosh, I have to go." He pointed a finger at her. "Thursday. One o'clock. I'll take care of lunch. Right?"

"Ah, erp, sure!"

"Great!" He flashed her a wink and backed toward the door, turning, finally, to hurry from the room.

Astonished, Cassidy flung an arm over the rolling rack. Then slowly her face crumpled. "Such a brilliant conversationalist, Miss Penno," she mocked in a nasal voice. "No wonder your brother doesn't trust you further than he can throw you backward through a hoop. Holy cow." She smacked herself in the forehead with the heel of her hand. First the glop and then the *ers* and *duhs*. And she had to have designs by Thursday! Thursday lunch!

Lunch with Paul Spencer. Holy cow!

Absently Paul tapped in the code that unlocked the driver's door of his sleek black Jaguar and slid beneath the wheel. Whatever had possessed him to insist on a luncheon date with Cassidy Penno? She was an engaging young woman, quite lovely even if she didn't know it—and he rather liked that she didn't—and fun in a way he hadn't encountered in a very long time. Her creativity and her wholesomeness were refreshing. None of that changed the fact that he was practically engaged to Betina. Practically but not quite, damn her.

Now, now, he chided himself, as he started up the engine and put the sleek auto in motion, *that's no way to think about your future wife.*

He was resolved, as his grandfather must have known he would eventually be, to making his stepcousin his wife. It was the only thing to do, really, considering that the scheming old man had left her thirty percent of Barclay Bakeries, the very same as he'd left Paul himself. Paul, of course, had another ten percent to go with his thirty, leaving thirty percent to be divided among other family members. His uncle Carl and his wife, Jewel, who was Betina's mother had ten. And so did his uncle John, who had never married, ten percent had gone to his deceased uncle's wife, Mary, and her daughter Joyce, who was now Joyce Spencer Thomas.

No nonfamily member had ever owned a share of the business, not since Paul's great-grandfather had founded it. Customarily, the spouses and children of family members shared in that member's legacy. However, both Paul's great-grandfather and grandfather had reserved huge majorities for themselves. The majority of the family had declined involvement in the business, content to pull in their financial rewards without bothering with the nasty details of enterprise.

Paul was the exception. He had a fine mind for business and a great desire to use it, and when he had ascended to the position of CEO upon his grandfather's retirement, he had foolishly assumed that eventually his grandfather's sixty percent majority would be added to the ten percent he had inherited from his own parents. Family tradition demanded it. The family themselves expected it, knowing that Paul could be trusted to guide the business with the same skill and dedication as his predecessors. Then the old man had thrown him a curve.

In truth, Paul partly blamed himself. He'd known for some time that his grandfather was concerned about his unmarried status. At thirty-eight, Paul was well past the age when most men married for the first time, but it wasn't for lack of interest. He just hadn't found the right woman. Perhaps she didn't really exist, this woman of his dreams—not that he could even assign her specific characteristics. He only knew that none of the many women with whom he'd involved himself had inspired in him the desire to be joined with her for life. Not even Betina.

He should never have allowed himself to be seduced by her. On the other hand, how many healthy, unattached men could resist a beautiful woman who walked into his office unannounced wearing nothing more than a hot pink raincoat belted at the waist, thigh-high stockings and three-inch heels? No, he couldn't be blamed for submitting to temptation, even if temptation's body had been surgically enhanced by the best plastic surgeons available. His true mistake had been in assuming that it was all in fun, and that the family at large would not assign significant expectations to what ought to have been private fun and games.

He couldn't prove that Betina had let the family in on what she had promised would be their secret, but he wouldn't put it past her. When he had realized that the family was ignoring his often-repeated assertion that his relationship with Betina was "casual," he had taken steps to put an end to the fun and games as well as the expectations. Privately Betina had expressed her perfect understanding of the situation. Publicly she had spent months dabbing unseen tears from her eyes every time he entered the room where she was or, apparently, his name was even mentioned. Paul found himself in the unpleasant position of having to reveal how the affair had started or enduring and hoping it would all eventually blow over. He'd thought it had blown over.

Oh, he was aware that much discussion had been devoted to the "suitability" of the pairing by the family at large, and on the surface it did seem perfect. Betina had been twelve when her mother had married Uncle Carl. Sixteen years later she was very much a part of the family fabric without actually being a member of the family, especially as Carl and Jewel had had no children of their own. Having her married to a bona fide member of the family must have seemed somehow poetic and his own lack of enthusiasm foolish if not downright

mean-spirited. On the surface Betina was the perfect woman—
lovely, accomplished, graceful, sophisticated, warm—but only
on the surface. Beneath the polished exterior, so far as Paul
could tell, was only a vast amount of ambition and a cold sort
of intelligence. Unfortunately he could not say as much to
anyone else in the family, except perhaps Joyce. But what
good would that do? Joyce was happily married to the plant
manager of the business, the bakery itself, and busy trying to
conceive a much-wanted first child.

If only he had explained in detail to his grandfather the
reasons for and extent of the affair, as well as his objections
to Betina herself as a wife, he might have spared himself and
the whole family their concerns. But he had played the gentleman—after playing the stud—and now he would pay for
the privilege. He had no choice. The family depended on him,
and Betina had revealed an alarming desire to meddle in business affairs. Worse, when thwarted, she had threatened to in-
volve the family in the fight, and that Paul could not allow.
He had pledged, literally, to protect the family from any un-
wanted involvement in the affairs of the company when he
had ascended to the position of CEO, and this sort of drama
was just what they feared most. And Betina had to know it.
So, despite months of looking for a way out, he was now
resigned to what he had to do. The problem was that he had
to do it before Betina's new marketing scheme could be put
into effect.

Disaster loomed on the horizon, especially as Betina had
chosen this particular moment, when Barclay Bakeries was
poised to expand into a national market, to bully him into
adopting the most ludicrous marketing gambit ever devised.
She wanted every slice of Barclay bread to be ''embossed''
with the image of Barclay's logo, the portrait of the fictional
Mrs. Barclay stamped in bread dough. The expense would be
exorbitant and the result ridiculous, but he had agreed, while
throwing up every roadblock to implementation imaginable, to

keep the family from being drawn into the fight. And he had, reluctantly, proposed marriage.

But Betina wanted her pound of flesh. She seemed determined to lead him a merry chase, to make him appear the besotted fool in front of the family. That was what this stupid costume party was really about. It had nothing to do, as she claimed, with keeping the business in the news. It was all an exercise in bringing him to heel. Well, he had a few tricks up his sleeve himself. And that was where Cassidy Penno came into the picture.

Which in no way explained why he'd felt compelled to make a date out of what should have been a bothersome business appointment. Now was not the time to be taking interest in another female. Nothing whatsoever could come of it. On the other hand, why shouldn't he enjoy himself if he could? Why should he give Betina the power to make him miserable? He would just make sure that Cassidy understood the situation. They were business associates who had the potential to become casual friends. That being the case, they were allowed to enjoy each other's company as long as they didn't get too personal. He could use a friend, and something told him that Cassidy could, too. But then, who couldn't?

So lunch was going to be a fun thing, nothing more, and he'd come up with a fun menu for it. He was enjoying himself just considering the possibilities. Almost-engaged men deserved to enjoy themselves. Even married men were allowed a bit of fun. Even men married to Betina Lincoln. *Especially* men married to Betina Lincoln, unless he missed his guess. And he was very much afraid that he didn't. Very much afraid.

Chapter Two

Cassidy chewed the inside of her cheek as she watched the caterers descend on her shop. They busily arranged a portable table covered by a sparkling white Damask tablecloth. She felt worried, thrilled and nervous all at once. Lunch, he'd said. It looked like a feast: fruit salad, an incredibly delicious-smelling beef Bourguignonne, crusty French bread; brie; wine; and for later, a chocolate gateau and whipped cream; all served by a uniformed waiter with a secretive smile. Cassidy smiled nervously in reply.

What could Paul Spencer be thinking? She was his costumer, sister to one of his employees, and nothing more. Yet he was treating her like a date, like someone in whom he was interested romantically. She wondered guiltily if William knew, and if not, should she tell him. Before she could come to any conclusion about that, Paul Spencer rushed into the room, speaking into a small cell phone.

"Yes, Gladys, I understand. Nevertheless, I am turning off the phone now, and I will not turn it on again until—" he checked his wristwatch "—two-oh-five." With that he punched a button, folded the phone into a palm-sized rectangle and dropped it into his jacket pocket, his gaze searching out Cassidy. When he spotted her, standing across the room beneath an artificial tree outlined with tiny white lights next to a gypsy caravan wagon and a campfire created with colored lights and fake logs, he smiled brightly.

Cassidy stepped forward, dismayed by the thrill she felt at seeing him again. She was making much too much of this, she told herself sternly. Paul Spencer was just a businessman doing what he deemed necessary to secure the service he needed. After all, it was the busy season for her, and she was doing him a favor because of his connection with William. He probably wined and dined all his business associates this way. She was probably the only one who fervently wished that he didn't. That in mind, she blurted, "You shouldn't have gone to all this trouble."

"No trouble," he said lightly. Then his gaze fell over the small, portable table carried in by the caterer, and he approached, rubbing his hands together with a smack of approval. "Looks good, and it isn't just because I'm starved."

Obviously pleased, the waiter immediately hurried around the table and pulled out a chair, waving Cassidy toward it. Selfconsciously, she stepped over the artificial campfire, knocking only one log out of place. Then she slid into the chair, with only a small bump against the corner of the table, resulting in shaking to the floor only a single salad fork, which the waiter snatched up and polished to cleanliness with a white cloth before carefully and reverently placing it once more next to its neighbor. Cassidy sat red-faced while the waiter performed the same courtesy with the chair for Paul Spencer, but without the slightest mishap. Paul settled himself and smiled across the table at her.

"I half expected to find you outfitted in green guacamole or some such."

The color of her face intensified. "Oh, no, I wouldn't wear a costume to lunch."

"Not even a costume lunch?"

His teasing relaxed her a bit, and she said, "I've never heard of a costume lunch."

"Well, we'll have to introduce it, make it the next big fad. Ought to be quite a boon for business." A grin quirked around the corners of his mouth, and Cassidy found herself laughing. "That's better," he said, leaning both elbows upon the table while the waiter fluttered about, lifting covers and spooning out portions.

Cassidy felt an acute shyness. No matter what she told herself, it felt as if she was being courted. But what would be the point in that? She had already agreed to help him with his costume. More important, the man was almost engaged to be married. Even if he wasn't, she couldn't quite imagine why he'd be interested in her. She was just a costumer and William Penno's younger, rather plain, sister. That in mind, she fixed her thoughts on business.

"Would you like to see my designs now?" she asked uncertainly, leaning back in her chair to allow the waiter to spread her napkin.

Paul waved a hand. "I'm too hungry to do anything just now but eat—and look at you."

"Oh." She resisted the urge to smooth her hair, knowing that it hung straight as a board right to the ends. After a moment she picked up her fork and began to eat her colorful fruit salad.

"Did you have a difficult time with it?" Paul asked, halfway through his salad already. "The design, I mean."

She put down her fork and dabbed her mouth with her napkin. "No, actually, I didn't. You're quite easy to imagine in costume."

"Is that good?" he asked, sounding hopeful.

She tried to find the words to explain, seeing in her mind's eye the way she'd pictured him during the course of her research. "Yes. You see, usually I picture characters in my costumes, and then somehow they don't look quite right on real people. Not to me, anyway."

"And you think I'll look the part?"

"Somehow I do." It was odd, really, but she'd been picturing him in quite a lot of costumes lately, and he'd looked splendid in them all—at least in her mind's eye. She shook her head.

"I imagine I will, then," he said, and she was aware of a tingling sense of pleasure at the soft words. He trusted her judgment. It shouldn't have pleased her so. It should have pleased William, though. The thought of anything she might do actually pleasing her rather uptight brother made her laugh, and Paul Spencer put down his fork, smiling as if he enjoyed the sound. "Why is it you lift my spirits?" he asked, parking his chin on his upraised palm.

"Me?" she heard herself say flirtatiously, and he smiled at her a long moment before picking up his fork again.

It was the most wonderful lunch of her life, and she told him so afterward.

"I wanted to do something special," he confessed, looking deeply into her eyes. She had the feeling that if Tony hadn't popped in just then, dressed as Charlie Chaplin, Paul would have kissed her, but then she was probably imagining things. They had a table between them, after all, even if it was a small table. The waiter had disappeared with the remains of their meal. Tony didn't bother with ceremony.

"Phone call for Mr. Spencer."

The intent look disappeared from Paul's face, replaced in swift sequence by irritation, disappointment and, finally, resignation. "I don't suppose you got a name?"

Tony's smile was somehow galling. "I didn't ask. It's a woman, though, if that helps."

A muscle ticked in the hollow of Paul's cheek. He rose to

his feet, speaking apologetically to Cassidy. "I'm sorry, but I'd better take it."

"Take your time," she said, getting to her own feet as the waiter returned, ostensibly for the table and folding chairs. "I'll be in the sewing room. Show him in, please, Tony, when he's ready."

Tony twitched his glued-on mustache and quickly doffed his bowler. Turning on his heel, he waddled away, feet aimed in opposite directions. Paul followed, the stiffness of his manner implying anger. Cassidy wondered at that, but then it really wasn't any of her business. Her business was costumes, and she'd best remember it. Sighing, she went off to the sewing room and began pinning her designs onto the bulletin board there for that purpose. Paul joined her in a surprisingly brief time, apparently unruffled.

He made no explanation about the call, but then she expected none. Instead, he looked around thoroughly and then approached the bulletin board, his hands clasped behind his back. He studied the drawings intently, his head turning this way and that. Once in a while he made an inquisitive sound. Otherwise, he betrayed nothing of his thoughts. After some time, he stepped back and looked at her.

"Do you have a favorite?"

The question surprised her. "Er, yes, actually I do. This one." She pointed to the center design. He stepped forward once more and studied that particular drawing. Then he nodded and stepped back again.

"When can we begin?"

"Begin?"

"Yes, I, um, assume fittings will be required."

"Of course, but—"

She had been about to say only one or two. He interrupted with an upraised hand. "Will Saturday work for you then, or would you rather not do it on the weekend? I'll understand, of course. I simply thought… That is, Saturday would be good for me."

She usually worked half days in the shop Saturdays—mornings. For some reason she said, "Saturday afternoon?"

He smiled, beamed, actually. "Excellent. Would you like to do lunch again?"

"Oh, no!" she said quickly, thinking of the expense he'd gone to. "I mean, that won't be necessary." He seemed a bit crestfallen, so she added, "We could have coffee here, though, if you like."

He smiled again. "All right, I'll see to it."

"No, no, let me," she insisted. "I-it's just coffee, after all."

"All right," he said. "Will three be suitable?"

"Three is fine," she told him, completely forgetting that she'd promised her mother a visit.

"Three then." He pointed at the design upon which they'd settled. "Good work. Thank you. I know it's an imposition for you at this busy time."

She shook her head. "I'm happy to do it."

He stepped close, one eyebrow arching, gaze intent on hers, saying conspiratorially, "Perhaps you ought to inform young Charlie then. He seems to think you're much too busy to be indulging in luncheons and extra work just now."

Cassidy gasped. Oh, that scamp! She closed her eyes in embarrassment and said shakily, "Young Charlie should learn to mind his own business." She would have to talk to Tony, again, not that it would do much good.

Paul chuckled. "I'd say he has a crush on you."

Cassidy rolled her eyes, muttering, "I should crush him."

"Now, now," Paul chided gently, his hand curled beneath her chin, tilting it slightly. "A boy's ego is a tender thing."

Cassidy burst out laughing. Only a man such as Paul Spencer could so adeptly put the matter into perspective. A boy, indeed, especially when compared with the man standing before her. "Maybe a good spanking, then."

Those blue-gray eyes darkened to the color of smoke. "Let's not encourage him," he said huskily, and again Cassidy sensed that he wanted to kiss her. For a moment she could neither breathe nor move, but then it passed, and he stepped away, his smile gone wry and tight, his hand falling to his side. "I have to go," he said.

She smiled to cover her disappointment. "You'll have to press the buzzer on Saturday. I lock the doors at noon."

"We'll be alone then?"

She had to swallow before she could answer. "Yes, alone." To her relief, her voice sounded nearly normal.

He smiled, softly this time, privately. "Saturday, then."

"Saturday."

She found herself smiling when he'd gone. She might be just a costumer, but he liked her, William Penno's sister or no, and it was terribly mutual. All too mutual. And it could come to nothing. He was as good as engaged to be married. Her smile faded to wistfulness. Then it occurred to her that she should have something ready for him to try on when Saturday came around—and she hadn't taken a single measurement! Well, she'd just have to do it on Saturday, which meant this thing was going to require a bit longer than it might have—and she didn't really mind, despite her full schedule. It was foolish, she knew. But when, she thought with a sigh, had she ever done the sensible thing? She should start, she knew, and she would...as soon as Paul Spencer was out of her life, which he would be all too soon.

The blustery, wet day was enough reason to stay indoors and cancel previous commitments, but Paul reminded himself that this was important. He told himself sternly it wasn't just that he wanted to see *her*. All right, she was interesting—a costumer, for heaven's sake!—and possessed of a quirky sense of humor. She was gentle, as well, and shy, almost painfully so at times, and pretty, in an unconscious, wholesome way that intrigued him. She seemed utterly without artifice, in itself a good joke, considering her occupation, which was what brought him out on a day like this—her occupation, that was.

Doggedly determined to keep this meeting brief, to the point and all business, he shook his hands free of his coat pockets and reached toward the buzzer. As if with a will of their own, however, his hands detoured to his head and smoothed back his dark hair. It had a tendency to wave and stick out in wet weather, and he was suddenly aware of an intense desire to look his best. When he realized what he was thinking, he burst out laughing. So much for "business"! He shook his head, wondering what it was about Cassidy Penno that made him feel like a boy with his first crush? His finger at last moved to ring the doorbell.

Several long moments went by before the shade in the window lifted and Cassidy Penno smiled out at him. The door opened, and she stepped back to let him in, quickly closing and locking the door again behind him.

"Hello," she said, reaching for the coat he was shrugging out of.

"Hi." He handed it over and watched as she carried it to the coat tree, standing between the counter and the door. The overhead lights were off, and the cloudy illumination let in by the big front windows was soft and misty, picking up the golden highlights in her thick hair, which she wore twisted up in back with long tendrils left to frame her face. She looked warm and welcoming in a pale yellow sweater set worn with black, slim-fitting jeans and brown half boots. Paul felt a lurch in his chest, and at the sight of her pale pink lipstick, his mouth went dry. Who was he kidding? This woman drew him like a magnet.

The old rage filled him, useless, impotent, and she sensed it at once, her sweet face going slack and troubled. "Is something wrong?"

He forced a grim smile and shook his head. "No." His

hands were shaking and cold. Rubbing them together, he thought of the coffee she'd promised him, and his mood lightened slightly. "I could use a hot drink."

She stepped back and swept him an elegant bow, one arm swinging out in invitation. "This way, good sir."

He laughed at her antics, feeling warmed just by her manner. He followed her through the darkened shop into the sewing room, smiling at the fanciful decorations along the way. Her mind seemed to teem with ideas and visions, which she obviously translated into actuality. He realized suddenly that he envied her that.

She had set up a table for them in one corner of the room. It was draped with what looked like an old paisley shawl trimmed with gold fringe and accented with a bouquet of decoratively folded lace handkerchiefs and old, silver teaspoons. In addition to a ceramic pot suspended over the flame of a tiny candle, she had placed on the table a pair of antique-looking cups and saucers, mismatched dessert plates, a creamer, sugar bowl and an intricately cut-crystal platter with a selection of mouth-watering pastries. Not a thing on the table matched another, and yet it all worked together with charming originality. Obviously she had gone to some trouble to indulge her creative bent in his honor, and he felt unaccountably touched.

"This is lovely," he said, lightly stroking the rim of one cup.

She had the grace to blush. "Thank you. The, um, coffee's flavored. I hope you don't mind."

"Not at all," he said, surprised to find that it was so. Normally he hated the pretentiousness of flavored coffees, but nothing about this particular woman was pretentious in the least, just the opposite, in fact. He indicated the pot. "May I?"

"Of course. Help yourself."

The aroma of amaretto seemed to fill the small room as he

poured a steady stream of hot black coffee into one of the cups on the table. He moved the spout over the second cup and looked up in question. Smiling, she nodded, and he poured a cup for her.

"Take anything with that?"

"Just a touch of milk."

He tilted the tiny milk pitcher over the cup and let a few drops trickle in, then stirred the brew to a rich brown before passing cup and saucer to her.

Reaching for a puffy chocolate muffin, he looked around for a chair. She had placed one at a slight angle, facing away from the drawing board to which it obviously belonged. She herself was hovering over a stool on rollers next to her sewing machine. He placed the muffin on a plate and handed it to her. She flashed him a smile of surprise. "Thanks."

"My pleasure." Choosing a sticky bun for himself, he pulled the chair close and sat down. The coffee tasted surprisingly rich and only faintly flavored. "Excellent," he said, placing the cup on the saucer and picking up the sticky bun. To his surprise he was ravenous, and he ate half the bun in one bite, polishing it off with the next. Swigging coffee, he looked over the serving platter again, torn between a strawberry tart and a little cake frosted with smooth white icing and decorated with a plump raspberry. He went for the tart, laughing when strawberry filling oozed out as he set his teeth into it. Cassidy laughed, too, and set aside her own goodies to come to his rescue with one of those absurdly delicate handkerchiefs. He wouldn't let her touch him with it, shaking his head and twisting aside as he licked the fingers that held the tart.

"You're going to get it all over you," she scolded playfully.

He grinned at her. "I'm a big boy. I can play with strawberry goo if I want to, one of the privileges of adulthood."

She laughed at that, too. "You may be grown-up, but you look like a little boy caught with his fingers in the jam jar."

He couldn't help himself. Dropping the tart to his plate, he reached out with his sticky hand and wiped strawberry "goo" onto the tip of her nose, chin, and cheek. Her mouth dropped open, and she danced back out of his reach before suddenly doubling over with laughter. Setting aside both plate and saucer, he went after her, catching her easily in one arm as she squealed and tried to defend herself with the handkerchief.

"This, Miss Penno," he teased, "is how little boys play with jam!"

Laughing and struggling, she twisted her body against him. Playfulness fled before a very adult surge of lightning-hot desire, and he found himself looking down into her upturned face, marveling, as she grew still, at how attuned she seemed to be to his every thought and mood. He pushed away the knowledge that he had no right to secure this young woman's affections and very deliberately wiped his sticky fingers across her mouth before lowering his head for surely the sweetest kiss he'd ever known. Her arms slid around his waist, holding him lightly as he forced her head back, licking and tasting and finally swirling his tongue around the inside of her mouth.

Gradually she pulled away and cleaned her face with the handkerchief. He saw in the bleakness of her moss green eyes that she knew what a foolish, pointless thing he had just done. "I'm sorry," he murmured, retreating to his chair.

"It's all right," she said softly, offering him another hanky.

He took it this time, smiling wryly. "No, it isn't."

She sighed. "Whatever you say."

He retrieved the cup and saucer, but had lost his appetite for the pastry. "I don't know what's wrong with me. I usually have better sense—and manners."

"You're probably just feeling trapped," she said off-handedly, wavering between her own disappointment and compassion for his obvious misery.

"You know don't you? I suppose William told you everything."

She shrugged. "He told me that your grandfather set up his will so that you have to marry a certain woman."

"Betina," he said bitterly.

"Betina of the Halloween costume party," Cassidy reminded him gently.

He smiled in spite of everything. She had such a way about her, this tall, slender, angelic woman. Meeting her had been the bright spot in the dark sky of his future, the oasis in the desert that had become his life, but that's all she could be, momentary, transitory, just a short stop along his way. She was right, of course, about him feeling trapped, and no doubt that had colored and intensified his every response to this woman. It wasn't fair, not to her and not to him and not to the marriage that he was obligated to try to build with Betina, but he'd be damned if he wouldn't enjoy his moments with Cassidy Penno. He had a right to that much, didn't he? So long as he didn't step over the line again. Mentally he drew that line boldly for himself: They could laugh together, talk together, work together, but there it stopped. He would not kiss her or touch her in a "romantic" fashion again. That gave him something to look forward to in the coming weeks but at the same time protected them both. His smile broadened. He drank his coffee and watched her drink hers.

Finally she set her cup aside. "We'd better get to work," she said, reaching for a blue plastic measuring tape, which she draped about her neck. Next she found a sheet of paper with a silhouette of the human body and lined brackets representing different measurements printed on it. She fixed the paper to a clip board and slid a pencil behind one ear, then positioned her stool in the center of the floor and motioned for him to stand before her. He did as she indicated, spreading his blue-jeaned legs slightly.

She wrapped the tape around his waist and snapped it apart again instantly before snatching the pencil from behind her ear and scribbling a notation on the paper. She measured his hips, legs, arms and shoulders in the same manner. "Man, you're good at this," he said, chuckling.

"Part of the job," she replied, then clamped the pencil between her teeth. "Wif oo ahms."

He laughed. "What?"

She took the pencil out of her mouth. "Lift your arms."

"Ah." He lifted his arms, and she wrapped the tape around his upper chest, pulling it tight in the center, her body moving close to his. The tape parted and slid free, but before she stepped back, he let his arms drop around her. She froze, and then she simply dropped down to the floor.

"Almost through," she said, as if he had not just tried to hold her.

Disappointment, relief, embarrassment and frustration percolated through him all at the same time. He ground his teeth. Obviously she had more sense and wisdom that he did. Just as obviously he couldn't trust himself with her. He waited for her to finish, but seconds ticked by and she made no move. When finally he looked down, it was to find her head bowed, her hands and the tape on the floor. Before he could say anything, she squared her shoulders, lifted her chin, and brought up the tape. As her hands rose slowly toward his groin, he realized in a flash that she had yet to take his inseam. In an instant he was hard as stone.

Catching her hands in his, he sank down with her on the floor. Placing her hands on his shoulders, he took her into his arms. Unresisting, she leaned forward awkwardly and laid her head on his shoulder. He placed his cheek against the top of her head and closed his eyes.

For a long while, he simply held her. The sudden rush of desire gradually faded, leaving in its place an odd sort of contentment tinged with sadness. He sighed and kissed the top of her head, saying, "I have no right to this. I can't change anything. The business is at stake, and my whole family's depending on me."

"I know," she whispered.

He ran his hands over her back, feeling the sharp little bumps that defined her delicate spine. Her breasts felt surprisingly heavy against his chest, given her small frame. He closed his eyes again, imagining her long, slender body lying alongside his. He could almost feel the jut of her hipbones, the softness of her flat belly, the firmness of the little mound at the apex of her thighs, her long legs tangling with his. "I wish I'd met you a long time ago," he said.

She lifted her head. "Before the affair, you mean."

He winced, loosening his embrace. "Will didn't leave anything out, did he?" He smiled at himself, at the irony of this whole thing, and teased gently, "I'll have to speak to him about that mouth of his."

She gasped and pulled away. "Oh, no, don't! He'll never understand. Please, Paul, don't—"

"Hey! It was a joke. I'm actually glad that he told you everything." His smile twisted wryly. "I'm not sure I could have. I think the temptation not to would have been too great."

He saw a spark of pleasure in her soft green eyes before she bowed her head again. Her fingers picked at the tape. "You just think that now. Probably if you didn't have this thing hanging over your head, you wouldn't even notice me."

"That's not true."

"Yes, it is," she insisted quietly. "It's all right. I'm used to it. I'm just not the sort men notice."

He laid his hand against the side of her throat and neck, feeling her pulse quicken. "What about Charlie Chaplin?"

She made a face. "Tony's not interested in me," she said firmly. "He just thinks that because I'm a virgin I must be frustrated enough to eventually give in if he keeps at me."

A virgin. Paul gulped. Heaven help him. When had he last met one of those? When had he even wanted to? What an utter fool he'd been, what a complete and total ninny to waste his time on experienced, sophisticated women when all this sweetness languished here. He'd played games when he might have had honesty and simplicity. He deserved just what he was getting. He deserved manipulative, scheming Betina. And Cassidy Penno deserved someone free to love and treasure her as the prize she was. He said, "Promise me you won't throw yourself away on the likes of that little imposter."

Her eyes grew round and then she burst out laughing. "On Tony Abatto?" she said. "I'd rather join an order of nuns!"

He chuckled. "Don't do that, either."

She sobered and told him solemnly, "Can't. I'm not Catholic."

They both erupted at that, laughing until their sides ached. Finally he got to his feet. When she started to do likewise, he pointed a finger at her. "You stay right there. Give me that measuring tape." Her gaze questioning but trusting, she did as he said. He pulled the tape through his fingers to the end, then placed the end at the place where his groin met his thigh. Pointing at the floor, he asked, "What does that say?"

She read the number, reached for the clip board and scribbled on it, muttering, "It says that you have very long legs."

"So do you," he said, imagining those legs wrapping around him. He cleared his throat, turning off the vision and said, "Okay, what's next?"

She took the tape from him and got up from the floor. "Fabric. We have to pick out fabric."

"All right," he said, caught up again in forbidden fantasies. He shook his head and belatedly added, "But, uh, not today. I, um, I have to get out of here. Go, I mean. I have to go." He glanced at his watch, trying to make it sound reasonable. "How about, um, Monday?"

She nodded, then said, "Listen, we don't have to drag this out if you don't want to. I can pick out the fabric and sew everything up, and we'll just do a single fitting, if you want."

He didn't want. He wanted every moment with her, but

maybe she was too smart to let him have it. He shrugged, surprised by how much it cost him. "Whatever you think best."

She looked away, pretending to be busy with the clipboard and pencil. "Oh, well, I usually prefer for the client to pick out the fabrics."

"Is that what you want," he asked carefully, "for me to pick out the fabrics?"

She turned her head one way and then another, looking at the figure on the paper, and then she dropped the clipboard and lifted her gaze to his. "Yes."

A giddy smile split his face. "Monday, then?"

She smiled, too. "Monday."

"What time?"

She bit her lip. "I close about six."

"Six," he repeated. They should have dinner. He wanted to have dinner with her, but he knew it would be stupid, beyond stupid, even risky, potentially devastating. He took a deep breath. "Would you like to have dinner with me afterward?" So much for being sensible. "I'll behave myself, I promise. Well, I'll try."

She gave him a slow, shy smile. "It would have to be someplace public, and maybe you wouldn't want to be seen—"

"I know just the place," he interrupted quickly. "It's nothing fancy, but the barbecue is great. You like barbecue?"

"I love it."

"Great! Okay, it's settled then. Monday at six; fabric first, then barbecue. I'll look forward to it."

"Me, too." They stood a moment, sharing the anticipation, before she said, "I'll walk you out."

He was careful not to touch her as they wound their way through the darkened shop again. At the front door she took his coat down and handed it to him. He slung it on and waited, telling himself that he simply could not give in to the impulse to kiss her goodbye. She slid open the dead bolt and turned the lock, depressed the thumb tab at the top of the curved handle and pulled open the door. The rain had ceased, but a chilly breeze gusted, blowing discarded paper and crisp leaves along the curb. He stepped out into dreary afternoon and turned back to face her.

"Thank you," he said simply.

She merely smiled and slowly closed the door. He turned and poked his hands into his pockets, inhaling deeply, breathing in and holding these last moments of freedom. He knew what he had to do and what it would cost him, but he also had Monday and perhaps a time or two after that. It would be difficult, even dangerous, and no doubt in the end he'd wind up with a broken heart, but he'd be damned if he wouldn't take every moment she'd give him. She deserved better, he knew, but he was cad enough to let her settle, in this case, for just what he could give back: some smiles, laughter, a little careful flirtation, the bittersweet knowledge that someone wanted her even if he couldn't have her. He wouldn't let it go beyond that. He would protect her from more, knowing that one day a man more deserving than he would gratefully receive all the treasure she had to give. He hated that unknown man already, but at the same time he wanted him for her.

God, who'd have thought straitlaced, uptight old Will could have a kid sister like Cassidy? He shook his head and strolled away in the direction of his car, content for that moment just to be amazed at the small ironies of life.

Chapter Three

They didn't waste any time with the fabric selection. Cassidy had put together several color-coordinated options, detailing how each fabric in each set would be used. She had them laid out on a table in the sewing room, alongside pencil-colored pictures showing how the costume would look. Paul glanced over them all and asked, "What's your favorite?"

She pointed to a particular combination of earth tones, blues and reds. He studied it about five seconds.

"Oh, yeah. That's definitely it. Let's go eat. I'm starved."

She laughed. "You're always starved."

"Lately," he said, realizing that his appetite had shown significant improvement during the past week. "Where's your coat?"

She went to a small door in one corner, opened it, and took out a man's navy blue wool, military-style, double-breasted coat. He hurried across the room to take it and hold it open for her to slip her arms into the sleeves. A name had been written on the inside label in red ink.

"C. Marmat," he read. "Who on earth is that?"

She shrugged. "Don't know. Some sailor who owned this coat before it went to the Army-Navy Store."

She buys her clothes secondhand at the Army-Navy Store, he marveled. Betina wouldn't touch even designer clothes on consignment. When he realized that he had actually compared the two of them, he shut down ruthlessly on the impulse. He had determined early that morning after a night of restless tossing to keep the two separate in his mind. Betina was his future, however dreaded. Cassidy was. . . his friend. He caught her by the hand and dragged her toward the showroom. Laughing, she tugged away, ran back to the closet and retrieved a minuscule purse on a long, thin strap. She slung the strap over her shoulder and ran back to him, placing her hand in his once more. Together they hurried through the store and out the front, which Cassidy locked with two separate keys.

Paul's car was waiting at the curb. He unlocked the passenger door and ushered her inside, then hurried around to slide beneath the wheel. The night was clear and pleasantly cool. As he drove them toward the barbecue place, Cassidy settled back into her corner and looked at him, one jeaned knee drawn up slightly so that the ankle of her burgundy boot lay against the edge of her seat.

"So, how was your day?"

He chuckled because it was the kind of thing long-term couples said to one another. "Okay. How was yours?"

"Oh, mine was fine," she said with a smug little smile. "I was Goldilocks today, and I made Tony be the baby bear. He was a very pouty baby bear."

Laughter spurted out of Paul's mouth. "Just how does a baby bear dress?" he wanted to know.

Cassidy's smile was sublime. "Well, he wears a bear suit, of course, and a pacifier on a ribbon around his neck and a diaper and a great big baby bonnet."

She painted a lovely picture, lovely enough to keep Paul laughing all the way to the restaurant, if *restaurant* was the

correct word. The place where Paul took her on lower Green-
ville Avenue was more of a supper club. The building was
slightly dilapidated with a neon sign out front that flashed and
buzzed, "Hoot Man's BBQ & Music Club." Even at six-
fifteen in the evening, a scratchy recording of jazz blared over
the loudspeaker by the door and a line of people snaked
around the side of the building. Paul parked at the side of the
building and pulled Cassidy by the hand around to the back
by the hand, where he pounded on a door labeled, Deliveries.

After several seconds the door opened, and a black man
wearing a spotless white apron greeted them. "Spence!" He
grabbed Paul's hand and pumped it energetically. "Hey, man,
why didn't you let me know you were coming?"

Paul grinned broadly. "Well, I thought I'd take my chances
for a change, but I see that the place is as popular as ever."

"We're hanging in there, man. We're hanging in." He
switched his gaze abruptly to Cassidy. "Who's this?"

Paul placed an arm around Cassidy's shoulders. "This is
my good friend, Cassidy Penno. Cass, this old scoundrel is
Hoot."

"Good friend, eh?" Hoot commented, nodding thoughtfully. "Like the coat."

Cassidy smiled. "Thanks."

Hoot spread out his arms. "Well, come on in!" He turned
and led the way down a long, narrow hall past a bustling
kitchen and a variety of other rooms to a small, dusty office,
where he put them in chairs and offered them drinks from a
small refrigerator in one corner.

"No, thanks, I'm driving," Paul said.

Cassidy smiled and shook her head, saying, "I don't drink
much."

Hoot sent Paul a significant look and sat down behind his
desk. Paul knew exactly what he was thinking. Paul didn't
drink much, either. Betina believed the "skill" of social drinking was a very important one and that he looked rude when

he repeatedly turned down offers of alcohol. He stopped short of pointing out to himself that Cassidy's feelings on the matter were much closer to his own.

Hoot templed his fingers over the top of his desk and asked, "How did you two meet?"

They both spoke at once. Cassidy said, "My brother works for Paul." Paul said, "Cassidy's my costumer."

Hoot latched onto that last. "Costumer! Costumer? As in Betina's infamous costume party?"

Paul made a face. "What else?"

Hoot clapped his hands together and boomed laughter. "You poor sucker!"

"I recall seeing your name on the guest list," Paul reminded him sourly.

"And do you have a costume, Mr. Hoot?" Cassidy asked brightly.

Hoot looked surprised, then his face split in that huge white grin of his. "It's just Hoot, no 'Mister,' and honey, I have the *best* costume. I plan to wear this big white apron here..."

"That he never gets dirty," Paul quipped drily.

"And a chef's hat," Hoot went on.

"Clever," Paul said.

"Cheap," Cassidy added. "Oh, and you should get one of those big oven mitts, too."

"Hey, good idea!" Hoot said.

"Do you have a chef's hat?" Paul asked, his brow furrowed in thought.

"No," Hoot admitted, "but I figure I can find one."

"Actually I'll be glad to rent you one," Cassidy said. "Five dollars."

His thick, woolly brows shot up. "That is cheap."

"I'll even throw in the oven mitt free. Now is that a bargain or what?"

Hoot looked at Paul. "She's sweet," he said. "Why don't you latch on to her and forget Betina the bi—"

"I don't think we want to go there," Paul said quickly, frowning.

Hoot linked his hands over a slightly protruding belly. "Hmph!" He looked at Cassidy. "It's that family of his. Bunch of leeches, if you ask me."

"Hoot."

He waved a hand to indicate that he considered Paul's protest so much spent air. "Long time ago there was a fight in the family over how to run the business, so they decided to pick a goat."

"Goat?"

"He means a scapegoat," Paul explained, "and he's way off base."

"The 'goat,'" Hoot said, "runs the business, and the rest of them go on their merry way, trusting him to take care of them all. He gets all the headaches, and they get nice fat checks dropped into their pockets at regular intervals."

"It gives me a free hand in running the business," Paul said.

"Is that the way you see it? Seems to me they tie your hands." He said to Cassidy, "They leave him out on a limb and pretend not to notice when someone else comes along with a saw. He can't vote their shares, and he can't ask them to vote with him. If he could, he could tell Hydra to take her marriage scheme and stick it—"

"Hoot!"

"All right, all right, I get it." He pointed at Cassidy. "This one's a lady. The other one is a she-devil."

Paul shot up to his feet, grabbing Cassidy's hand. "I've had this lecture already, and I'm starved. Do you mind if we eat here, or would you like to ruin the rest of my evening, too?"

Hoot rolled his eyes. "Dinner's on me."

"Thanks," Paul drawled wryly.

Hoot got up and smiled at Cassidy. "You give that chef's hat to the goat here, and don't forget to charge him for it."

She laughed. "I'll do that. Nice to meet you, Mr—" he glowered, and she amended "—Hoot."

He smiled. "We've got a honey-roasted barbecued chicken breast that ought to be sweet enough for you, sugar." As Paul pulled her from the room, he added, "Tell 'em to give the goat sauerkraut and barbecued sausage links!"

Cassidy giggled, flowing along in Paul's wake. "He's really a very nice man," she said.

"Yes, he is," Paul agreed grudgingly. Suddenly he stopped, shoved her up against the wall, plastered his body to hers, and tilted her chin up with his hand. She knew what was coming and did nothing to stop him. He kissed her very deliberately, drawing it out as long as he could bear to. When he pulled back and looked down into her face, she showed him everything he could ever hope for. Her eyes were closed, and her pretty mouth was curved in a gentle, dreamy smile. He laid his forehead against hers and whispered, "Why did you let me do that?"

She sighed. "I couldn't help it."

He closed his eyes, thinking, *Neither could I.* But he had to. It wasn't fair to either of them to let it go beyond friendship. He took a deep breath, opened his eyes and stepped back. Her smile remained gentle, understanding. He felt a wringing desperation, a sense of incomparable loss. He caught her hand again and led her down the hall to a black door. They went through it into a large dark room, buzzing with the noise of many people. A man at an upright piano in the center of the room played a meandering, almost desultory tune as if he were in a room alone and greatly bored.

Paul led her through a warren of tables and chairs of every description to a dark place behind a square column. "This is the treats table," he said as he helped her out of her coat and hung it on the back of her chair over the strap of her handbag, then shrugged out of his own and stuck it on a single hook protruding from the wall above and behind him before taking the chair opposite her. "You sit here by invitation only. That way the waiters and waitresses know you aren't to be charged for your meal."

"That's brilliant."

"I think so." A candle in a tin can sat at the edge of the table against the wall. Some matchsticks lay scattered around it. Paul struck one and lit the candle. Light streamed out of dozens of tiny holes piercing the tin can. He looked around them.

"What do you think?"

"About the restaurant? Interesting. I never thought of shabby as a decorative theme, though."

He chuckled. "Hoot wants the place to feel comfortable, to evoke one of those hole-in-the-wall places where the only draw is the wonderful food."

She nodded. "Well, he seems to know what he's doing."

"Umm-hmm."

They sat in silence for a moment before an obviously harried waitress in jeans and a halter top appeared. "Hey, Paul."

"Eileen. The place is certainly hopping tonight."

"Every night," she said. "What'd you do to induce the boss to treat you?"

Paul grinned. "Let him insult me and stick his nose into my business."

"Oh, he's good at that," she declared.

Paul reached across the table and took Cassidy's hand. "This is Cassidy Penno, Eileen. Hoot says she's to have the honey-roasted chicken breast."

Eileen's eyes went wide. "What'd you do to rate the private specialty?"

"It's an off-menu item," Paul explained. "They don't even tell you about it unless Hoot gives his permission first."

Cassidy inclined her head, signaling that she was suitably impressed. She said to Eileen, "I offered to rent him a chef's hat."

"A chef's hat?" Eileen's confusion was evident. She looked at Paul, but he just looked back at her. After a moment she shrugged, bent her head and scribbled the order on a pad. "One honey-roasted barbecued chicken breast dinner. Anything else?"

Cassidy grinned at Paul. "I think you were supposed to have the sauerkraut."

Paul grimaced and said to the waitress. "Make it two."

"Two honey-roasted barbecued chicken dinners. What'll you have to drink?"

"Iced tea."

"Same."

"I'll have it out in a jiff." She looked at Paul and added, "Hey, Paul, play something, will you? That guy's boring me to tears."

Paul laughed and said, "Okay."

The waitress turned and hurried away, stopping by the piano to speak to the guy there. He got up and left without a qualm. Paul got up and pulled Cassidy up with him. "Come on. The least I can do is play for my supper."

Cassidy trailed him to the piano in the center of the room. He parked her on one end of the bench and sat down next to her. Flexing his fingers, he began to play a raggy version of "Old Man River." Again, Cassidy was suitably impressed. Before he was through, the room had gone silent, and she was hanging on his arm, fascinated. He felt inspired and segued right into a soulful rendition of "Dixie," followed by a jazzy interpretation of "Amazing Grace." Eileen came by, left their dinners on top of the piano and stayed long enough to lean on her elbow, sigh and tap her toes a few times. He got up to applause, including Cassidy's, and acknowledged it with a series of quick bows before helping her carry their dinners back to the table. His mood had mellowed. For the moment at least, all was right with his world. He knew, too well, that he couldn't ask for more.

* * *

Cass leaned back in the car seat and groaned with contentment. She was stuffed to the gills. The food had been fabulous. She had been kissed in a hallway by a fabulous man, who had then played her three fabulous songs and flattered her with his eyes the rest of the evening. A night to remember, she told herself, fully aware that she was falling in love with the wrong man.

Did it happen like this often? she wondered. She didn't think so. Never before had she just met someone and felt inexorably drawn to him. It was as if they fitted together like a hand in a glove or pieces of a puzzle. Naturally he would be practically engaged to someone else, someone he didn't love but must marry. It wouldn't happen any other way with her. She had never for a moment believed that it would happen any other way, that she would meet the perfect man, love him and have him, too. It was Paul for whom she felt sorry, Paul for whom her heart broke. He turned his head away from the windshield momentarily to look at her.

"Why don't you let me take you home? I'll send someone to the shop for your car."

"Don't be silly," she said. "I'll be fine. I've been going home alone for a long time now."

"Still," he said, "I don't like it. At least let me follow you to be sure you get there okay."

She smiled. "All right, you can follow me."

He relaxed. "Good."

A few minutes later she was driving her ancient compact convertible west on Woodall Rogers, then south on Interstate 35 to her little house in Oak Cliff. Paul's luxury car followed right behind her. When she pulled into the drive of her small house, Paul pulled over to the curb and waited until she let herself in, turned on the living room light and waved to him. Then he pulled away from the curb and moved on down the street. She went inside, locked the door, threw off her coat and picked up the yellow cat rubbing against her ankles.

"Hello, Sunshine. Did Granny Anna come by to feed you earlier? Did she stay to keep you company for a little while, hmm?" Sunshine meowed and rubbed his head under her chin. She carried him into the kitchen, where "Granny Anna" had left a note taped to the refrigerator. The refrigerator, according to Cassidy's mother, Anna, along with the rest of Cassidy's house needed "purifying." In addition to teaching Tai Chi, Anna had recently taken up the study of attaining balance in one's surroundings through various Oriental rituals and principles. Anna promised to be as ardent about this new "discipline" as she was about vegetarianism, healthful exercise, her own version of the work ethic and gardening. Not to mention her concern for her children and her criticism of their father, her ex-husband, Alvin, who at sixty had joined a motorcycle "gang" and grown a ponytail despite the fact that he had no hair on the top of his head. Cassidy sighed, wondering how much "purifying" she was going to have to endure in order to placate her mother.

Her door bell rang. Cassidy glanced at the digital clock on the microwave. Almost nine-thirty. Who could be calling at this hour? She let down the cat, tiptoed into the living room and peeked out the spy hole in the door. Heart leaping, she threw the bolt and ripped open the door. Paul stood with his forearms braced against the opening.

"Paul? Uh, c-come in."

He shook his head, face serious. "We shouldn't...we didn't agree when to meet next."

"Oh! The first fitting. Well, let's see. How's Thursday? No, better make it Friday. Friday okay with you?"

"No," he said flatly. "It's too far away."

She was thrilled, of course, but it would be Friday before she could get together something for him to try on.

"Have breakfast with me Wednesday morning," he said, "and we'll do the fitting on Friday. Okay?"

"B-breakfast?"

His mouth began to curve up into a smile. "That's all that's left, isn't it? We've already had lunch, coffee and dinner."

She laughed. "Breakfast it is. Where and when?"

"Seven too early?"

"Seven's fine."

"How about if I just bring it with me?"

"Here, you mean."

His expression grew serious again. "Unless you think it's too risky."

She smiled, knowing that he was trying to protect her and that it was useless. It was already much too late for that, but it would not only be stupid but cruel to tell him that. She said, "Why don't I just cook for us? I can scramble an egg, you know."

He laughed at that. "I'm not surprised, but keep it simple, okay? Cold cereal and milk will do me fine."

"I think I can do a little better than that," she said.

He cocked his head, his grayish eyes suddenly smoky. "It's not the food, you know," he told her. "It's the company I'm after."

"Thank you."

"What for?" he asked ruefully. "Complicating your life?"

She shook her head and reached out to stroke his jaw with the backs of her fingers. "Just for showing up in it."

"Won't be for long," he said softly, his smile growing bitter.

"I know," she told him, "but that's all right. Better a little time than no time at all."

He reached out for her with a moan that was part pain and part gratitude. She moved into his arms as easily as if she'd done it a million times. He pressed his cheek against hers and held her close for a long while. Finally he pulled back, saying, "Gee, I'm a selfish bas—"

She laid her fingers across his mouth. "No, you're not. You're just helpless, and I know how that feels."

He cupped her face in his hands, kissed her lightly on the mouth, and quickly stepped back out of reach. "Good night."

She closed the door at his back and locked it again. Then she wrapped her arms around herself and closed her eyes. Her mother often told her that she was a glutton for punishment, a natural victim. She had never been so glad that her mother was right.

Anna *would* show up when the kitchen was full of the smell of bacon grease and smoke. She came in the back door, plunked down her woven grass bag and put her hands to her hips in a familiar, combative pose. Her long, gray hair lay in a loose braid across one shoulder. She wore a man's old dress shirt and T-shirt belted over a long, gathered skirt, with high-top tennis shoes. "What are you trying to do," she demanded, "burn down the house or poison yourself?"

"I'm trying to make breakfast for a friend," Cassidy said, blowing hair out of her eyes.

"You poison your friends?" Anna asked. "Why can't you understand that eating dead things kills you?"

I should eat live things? Cassidy wondered, but she kept her tongue tucked firmly behind her teeth. Arguing was one of the things Anna did best, arguing and deduction.

Her mother wandered around the room, pausing occasionally to sniff and pose with hands outstretched as she felt for vibrations. "It's a man," she said with some shock. "You're having a man in for breakfast!"

"I'm having a friend in," Cassidy said, carefully stirring the gravy while checking the biscuits in the oven.

"A *man* friend," Anna insisted.

"Well, it isn't as if I haven't had men friends before," Cassidy pointed out.

"For breakfast?"

Cassidy rolled her eyes. "He didn't spend the night here, Mom, if that's what you're implying."

"You know I don't imply things," Anna said truculently. "I speak my mind. Life is too short for implications and hints and—"

"Yes, yes," Cassidy interrupted, "I completely agree. Did you want something specific?"

"I left you a note," Anna pointed out.

Cassidy sighed. "Fine, fine. Purify away, just not this morning, all right?"

"I'll ask Kai Phong for a horoscope reading and make an auspicious appointment. You'd best not be here. Your negative energy would screw up his readings."

"Just let me know when you want me to be absent from my own home," Cassidy grumbled.

"Ah, there's my grandcat," Anna said, clapping her hands happily as Sunshine swayed into the room. She bent over and made kissing sounds at the cat, who made her way regally to Cassidy and rubbed against her legs before leading her plumed tail in Anna's direction. "Come here, shweetheart, and wet Gwanny hold wou."

Sunshine deigned to be fawned over. Anna closed her eyes, the cat tucked up under her chin. "We have such a strong connection," she said to no one in particular. Cassidy smiled, her back to her mother. Anna was always hinting that Sunshine should have been her cat instead of Cassidy's, and Cassidy always pretended not to understand. The fact was that the cat had shown up on Cassidy's doorstep one day. Cassidy had taken it in and run ads in the Dallas paper in case someone was looking for it, but no one had claimed the cat, and she had adopted it. Anna believed that the cat had actually come in search of her, as some sort of benevolent earth spirit seeking its human equivalent.

The buzzer on the oven and the doorbell rang at the same time. Cassidy turned off the burner under the gravy and started to the door, then turned back and switched off the oven. She started for the door a second time, but she was undecided about the biscuits, whether they should be left in the oven to keep warm or taken out before they could overbake. She went back and yanked the biscuits out of the oven. Anna was at the door before she got halfway across the living room.

"How do you do, young man. I'm Anna, Cassidy's mother, and this is her cat, Sunshine."

Paul leaned sideways slightly and looked over Anna's shoulder to Cassidy. She lifted a hand in a limp hello and smiled apologetically. His own smile was warm and welcoming. He switched his attention back to Anna and the cat. The cat got a little scratching behind the ears. "I'm Paul Spencer. Ah, may I assume that you are William's mother, as well?"

Anna rocked back on her heels. "You know my son, William?"

"Yes, um, we work together."

Anna turned sideways and looked at Cassidy in surprise. "Did you know that he works with your brother?"

"Yes. Actually, in a way, William introduced us."

Anna shook her head. "This is very strange, very strange." She swung a narrowed gaze in Paul's direction. "When is your birthday, young man?"

Paul seemed taken aback, but he answered politely, "January seventh."

Anna tapped herself on the chin, muttering, "January seventh, January seventh, hmm. I'll have to check this out." She put down the cat, cooed to it and swept past Cassidy into the kitchen. She reappeared a second later with her grass bag in tow and pointed at Paul Spencer. "If you eat dead things, you'll die," she pronounced sagely, and then she was gone.

Cassidy heard the back door click shut behind her. She looked at Paul and knew at a glance that he was trying desperately not to laugh. Her own laughter sputtered out, and then the two of them met in the center of the room, howling, their arms thrown around each other.

"I'm sorry," she said, finally pulling away to close the door and take his coat, "she's very...very..."

"Unique?" Paul suggested.

Cassidy giggled. "New Age." She sobered again and sighed, adding, "She means well."

Paul followed her into the kitchen, nodding. "Has anyone told her that we'll die no matter what we eat?"

Cassidy grinned, then abruptly felt guilty about it. "She's right, though," she said, "some things just aren't good for you."

Paul walked over to the stove, sniffing appreciatively. "Like bacon and eggs and biscuits and—" he smiled unrepentantly "—gravy? Real homemade gravy?"

Cassidy couldn't help smiling with pleasure. "My grandmother taught me."

He picked up a plate from the kitchen countertop and began filling it. "My blessings on dear old Grandma."

She went to the cabinet, took down a cup and poured it full of coffee for him, placing it on the table. "Um, you don't eat like this all the time, do you?"

"Hardly ever," he said over his shoulder.

She sighed with relief. "Good. That's pretty much what I thought."

"Did you? Why?"

"You're so fit," she said baldly.

He turned away from the stove then, his plate piled high. "I try. Thanks for noticing."

She blushed. Of course she'd noticed. Every time he put those strong arms around her and pulled her against her hard body, she noticed. Noticing kept her awake nights. He ate off his plate as he walked toward the table, saying between bites, "What kind of workout do you do?"

"Workout?"

He set down the plate and let his eyes slide over her. "Don't tell me that body's a gift of nature."

Her blush intensified. Her fingertips fluttered over her black leggings and sweater. "I, uh, well, I power walk three or four times a week."

"Oh, that's good. You don't play racquetball or anything like that, do you?"

"No."

"Want to learn?"

Was he asking to teach her to play racquetball? "Sure."

He smiled and pulled out his chair. "Great. Now are you going to join me?"

She filled her own plate judiciously and joined him at the table. Later, on his way back to the stove for a refill, he said, "Has your mother always been, well..."

"Weird?" Cassidy supplied.

"I didn't say that."

"You didn't have to. And no, she's hasn't always been this way. I mean, she was always opinionated and outspoken, but she didn't get into the other stuff until after she and Dad divorced."

"I see. That explains how you turned out so normal."

"Me? Normal?"

"You don't think you're a healthy adult female?" he asked, sounding surprised.

"Not according to my family."

"No? Well, you have to consider the source. Take your mother. She is a little, um..."

"Weird."

"Left of center, I was going to say."

"Way left."

"I don't know your father," he went on, "but William's a stuffed shirt, if you'll forgive my saying so."

"Uptight, you mean."

"Majorly."

She shook her fork at him as he sat down again. "Let me tell you about dear old Dad. He's into fun. That's why he divorced my mother, she wasn't any fun, and she didn't want him to retire early so he could have his own fun.''

He chuckled and shook his head at that. "Dad sounds like my favorite already.''

"Um, he's very worried about me.''

"Oh? How come?''

"Because I'm a twenty-five-year-old virgin.''

He went perfectly still, and then he laid down his fork and templed his fingers over his plate. "What's wrong with that?''

"According to my father it shows a marked inability to loosen up and have a little fun, which—again, according to my father—should be one of life's priorities.''

"There are more important things than having fun,'' he told her solemnly.

"Yes, I know. My mother tells me so constantly.''

"I believe in making things count,'' he went on. "Whether it's fun or work—''

"Or sacrifice?'' she said.

He lowered his hands, curled them into fists, relaxed them again. "Yes, even sacrifice.''

"Tell me about Betina,'' she said, and surprisingly he did.

After telling the story, he ended with, "I could almost be flattered she's gone to such great lengths, if I thought for a moment that it was anything on her part but greed and pique and wounded pride.''

Cassidy said, "I'd never have enough nerve to do any of that.''

He shrugged. "Who can say what any of us could do if we had to? I think you're pretty brave, sitting here with me, knowing what you know.''

"Brave or stupid,'' she quipped.

He frowned. "Not stupid, definitely not stupid.''

"No, not that,'' she said softly, "just too late or something.''

He took her hand in his, squeezing it. "I'd change it all if I could."

"I know."

"Listen," he said, dropping his gaze, "I'll go away and never come back again if that's what you want."

"It isn't."

He looked up at that, his grip on her hand almost painful. "I'm so glad. I don't know how to explain it, except to say that I need you as my friend right now."

"We're not friends, Paul," she told him gently. "None of my friends ever kissed me like you do."

He let go of her hand. "And that has to stop," he said grimly.

"It won't," she told him, and to prove it, she leaned forward and put her mouth to his.

Chapter Four

He didn't feel nearly as ridiculous as he should have, and he knew that he had Cassidy to thank for that—and so much else. Tony Curtis he was not, but he made a credible Cossack or some such thing and, unlike the spaceman in the corner and the headless half of a horse sitting on Betina's spotless white sofa, his costume was as comfortable as his usual clothing. He wet his lips with the tepid champagne in his glass and smiled obediently as Betina signaled him from across the room.

Gritting his teeth, he made his way carefully through the chatting, laughing crowd, holding his drink aloft as he jostled past Marie Antoinettes and clowns, wolves and shepherdesses, vampires and pumpkins. Betina was dressed as a fairy princess. She was going to need real magic to clean her absurd white carpet and upholstery after this. Well, that was her problem. She would have another if she thought she was going to replace the warm colors in his Park Cities home with her cold whites. Aside from the costumes, most of which were downright garish, the only color in the well-lit room came from the pot plants and the tinges of yellow in the walls and pink in the draperies. He reached her side, elbowing past a roaring-drunk George Washington to smile benignly at the scantily clad prehistoric couple to whom she introduced him.

"Macie and Marc Gladsden, this is Paul Barclay Spencer of Barclay Bakeries."

He was always Paul Barclay Spencer of Barclay Bakeries to Betina. Were he plain Paul Spencer, he wouldn't be standing here playing the whipped puppy for her. "Hello."

The Gladsdens looked him over as if he were a piece of meat. He kept his face impassive and sipped champagne, while Betina pretended that Macie wasn't staring at his crotch. He knew exactly what was going on here. The Gladsdens were part of a wild crowd. He'd heard tales of wife swapping and orgies. A lot of Betina's friends visited the wild side, the wild side of high society, mind, but the wild side, nonetheless. Whenever anyone told her about one of those friends of hers, she always pretended shock, but he never noticed that she dropped anyone. Then again, she wouldn't. It simply wasn't politic. He, on the other hand, generally refused to mix socially with the wild crowd, and in her book that made him the greatest hypocrite. All things considered, maybe she was correct about that, but he still reserved the right to pick his own friends—and always would. At the moment, however, he had little choice but to endure.

Conversation was desultory, but Betina was apparently satisfied with civility on his part. After several minutes—not too quickly, of course—she rescued him by slipping her arm through his and steering him off in another direction, saying, "Oh, there's Samantha Bishop in a perfectly awful Indian getup. If I know her, she won't stay ten minutes and will go home offended if I don't say hello."

So began a promenade around the perimeter of the room, Betina calling all the shots, him demonstrating that he'd been brought firmly to heel. He was actually glad to see William Penno dressed as Daniel Boone, complete with flintlock rifle.

Betina left him in William's care, saying, "Entertain your boss, Penno. The hostess can't afford to be monopolized."

Penno actually replied, "Yes, ma'am," in a tone that implied he'd been greatly honored. Penno's obsequiousness amused Paul more often than not, and he was good at his job, even if he was an absolute bore.

"If I may say so, Paul," William commented lightly, "you look just fine." It had taken Paul eight months to convince Penno that he really didn't want to be called sir, but William always let him know that he would never presume that first names made them friends. Poor William never could understand that being a genuine friend would make him many more points with Paul than constantly demonstrating his willingness to forever be a subordinate. How was it that William's sister could so naturally be his opposite? A hand extended in friendship to Cassidy Penno was a hand received in friendship. Somehow he knew that about her without having to be told.

He smiled at William. "Why, thank you, Will, and thanks, by the way, for sending me to your sister."

"Oh, no," William said, protesting gently, "thank you for allowing us to be of service."

Paul made a conscious effort not to roll his eyes and asked, "Did she choose your costume for you?"

"What? Oh, actually, no," William said. "She supplied it, of course."

"Of course."

Paul couldn't help wondering if Cassidy might not have chosen something a little more, well, William, like a court page or a butler. He chuckled at the notion, thinking he'd have to run it by Cassidy to see if her reaction was the same.

Conversation waned, but Paul didn't really mind. He hated the canned small talk that so many people seemed to think was required of them in a social situation. He much preferred silence if honest discourse was impossible, and too often it seemed that it was.

All too soon, Betina returned to claim him again, this time with an older couple in tow. The husband quickly announced that he'd thought this costume stuff was a bunch of hooey, but it had turned out to be a lot of fun. The wife gushed on and on until Paul thought he was going to have to locate a pair of hip boots. He knew it was all a test of his willingness to prostrate himself at her feet when Betina announced baldly that she had a marvelous idea.

"A costume ball! It will be the business coup of the year!"

Those words *business coup* set off fire alarms in his head, but he stayed calm while she elaborated.

"Think of it, we can invite the local *and* national distributors *and* our wholesale customer reps. We could do it New Year's Eve, so it can be like the kickoff for our new distribution plan!"

Very thoughtfully Paul said, "A party that size will be expensive."

"But think of the publicity!" Betina exclaimed, obviously already having done so. "Not to mention the good will and the face-to-face contact. We could block out a couple days before and after for our guests to book appointments with you personally."

He had to admit that there was some merit in that part of the plan. Finding time and opportunity to meet with everyone with whom Barclay did business was very difficult. How much more difficult would it be once they went national? A lot. But why a costume ball? Why not just a big party? Suddenly he knew the answer to that, and it was strictly personal. He tried to keep his enthusiasm in check, knowing that Betina would pounce on it as quickly as his reluctance.

"Actually," he said, "William can help us with this."

William got that caught-in-the-headlights look. "Me?"

Paul shrugged. "Someone will have to supply the costumes, and it seems to me that it would be asking a lot of our guests to expect them to fly in from all over the country with costumes in tow. Some of these things require crates for storage.''

A look of understanding lit William's face, then doubt set in. Before he could wonder aloud whether or not his sister could handle something of this size, Paul said, ''William's family owns the largest costume shop in the city. Isn't that right, Will?''

''Uh, well, technically, it's my sister's—''

''Great place!'' Paul went on, careful to praise the shop and not Cassidy. ''They do it all, designing, sewing, fitting. They've got thousands of costumes in stock. I wonder if there's any kind of master list, you know, what they've got in what sizes.''

''Oh, yes, actually, there is. I advised Cassidy on the sort of computer setup necessary for just such records.''

''Well, you'd be the man for it,'' Paul said, clapping him on the shoulder hard enough to make the stock of the long rifle clasped upright in his hands hit the floor. ''Tell you what, let's you and I talk to your sister about it first thing Monday morning…unless you think that won't be possible.''

''Oh, no! I'm sure Cassidy will be glad to talk to us. In fact, I'll arrange it myself.''

''You do that,'' Paul said, sipping his champagne again to hide the smile quirking at the corners of his mouth.

''Well,'' Betina said, crossing her arms and waving her wand above her head, ''I'm pleased to see that you're not going to fight me on this, Paul. You see, I do have good ideas.''

Paul nodded, smiling, all too aware that the older couple were hanging on every word and gesture. Betina went off to report her latest victory to anyone who might conceivably be interested, while Paul watched William begin to sweat. After a bit, William leaned to one side and whispered into Paul's ear, ''Sir, er, Paul, are you quite certain my sister's little shop can handle this? Maybe we ought to investigate a national chain. There are a few, you know."

"Think a national chain will be interested in accommodating us on such short notice, Will?" Paul asked softly. "After all, we've less than two months to pull this off. I don't suppose Betina thought of that, do you?"

William sucked in a mortified breath. "Two months! Oh, god. I know my sister, and she's—"

"Exactly what we need," Paul interrupted smoothly. *Exactly what I need,* he amended silently. Without knowing it, Betina had given him the perfect excuse to continue seeing Cassidy Penno, and it was entirely legitimate.

He managed to avoid private conversation with Betina for the remainder of the evening, which was good, since his mind was working furiously on this costume ball idea. The more he thought of it, the more he wondered if Betina had any concept of what was involved here. It was too late to book any type of room for New Year's Eve. Just the organization of such an undertaking could take weeks. What about food, decorations, invitations, transportation? Hotel rooms! He began to doubt that it was possible to get this thing together, but he kept that doubt to himself. Betina would be the one to have to call this off, and until she did, he would have plenty of excuses to meet with Cassidy. He'd see to that himself.

It was near midnight when the telephone rang, but all Cassidy had to do to answer it was roll over and lift the receiver. She hadn't slept a wink. She kept wondering how the party had gone and if Paul was now formally engaged to Betina Lincoln. He hadn't exactly said so, but Cassidy sensed that once he became formally engaged, their relationship, whatever it was, would end. She put the receiver to her ear and said, "Hello."

"Cassidy?"

"Paul?"

"I know it's late, but this is important."

"It's all right," she said, reaching up to switch on the bedside lamp and struggling into a semisitting position. "What's up?" She closed her eyes, anticipating the worst.

Instead of *I can't see you anymore* he said, "I need your help."

She opened her eyes and leaned forward to rest her forearms against her knees. Sunshine stretched at the foot of her bed and yawned before going into her imitation of a dead cat, lying on her side, legs thrust out stiffly. Cassidy said, "You know I'll do anything I can."

"Yes," he said softly. "I'm counting on it."

She cradled the telephone receiver in both hands. "So tell me what I can do."

"I'm not exactly sure yet," he said, "but I know it's going to take lots of meetings to get it done."

She dropped her legs flat on the bed. "I don't have the foggiest idea what you're talking about."

He chuckled. "I got clobbered with the idea of a New Year's Eve costume ball for Barclay Bakeries' business associates tonight, and I more or less instructed your brother to set up a meeting with you to discuss the matter."

"*This* New Year's Eve?"

"I knew you'd grasp the significance of that little detail immediately."

"Paul, I don't think it can be done."

"That's Betina's problem," he told her. "I'm just helping out with the costumes."

"Ah." She finally got the message. He'd leaped at Betina's preposterous suggestion as a legitimate means by which to continue seeing *her*. She was both relieved and worried. She had to ask. She took a deep breath and did it, "Paul, did you ask Betina to marry you again tonight?"

"Hell, no!"

Cassidy wilted back into a supine position, weak with relief.

If he hadn't asked, then Betina couldn't have accepted, which meant that he wasn't formally engaged—yet. "I really thought... That is, I expected... I mean, William said you were trying to win her back. I thought that was what tonight was all about."

After a short silence, Paul said, "Cassidy, there isn't a romance between Betina and me, not on my part, not on hers. Betina's too smart for that. She knows that I don't love her. I know that she doesn't love me. No one's trying to 'win' anyone."

"But I think—" Cassidy bit her lip, uncertain that her thoughts would be welcome. She needn't have worried.

"What? You think what, Cass?"

"I-I know you say that she doesn't love you, Paul, but she must have some feeling for you. If all she wanted was money or influence or power, she has that in Barclay stock."

"Yes, I know, but what she doesn't have is full, legitimate entry into the family, and salve for her pride."

"I can understand the first, I think," she told him honestly, "but how does forcing you to marry her salve her pride?

"She set out to get me, Cass," he said simply, "one way or another. All she wants now is just to know that I've accepted my fate and will make the best of it."

Cassidy sighed. "My stars, Paul, that's the saddest thing I've ever heard."

"No, Cass," came the soft reply, "the saddest thing is loving someone you can never have."

She dared not say another word for fear that he would reveal she was his "someone"—or she would reveal that he was hers. But he was right. The sadness that filled her was bottomless and black. She said, "We need to try to get some sleep."

"All right. Good night."

"Good night, Paul."

"I'll see you soon?"

"See you soon," she confirmed and hung up the phone.

Surprisingly, sleep came quickly this time. It stole in silently as she held the thought in her mind that it wasn't over yet. They could be "more than friends" for a little while longer.

William turned off the cellular phone, folded it and gave it back to Paul. "Betina says about three hundred, and Gladys feels that she can have the invitations out in a matter of hours, once the details are nailed down." He smiled self-deprecatingly, his way of saying that he told them so. "This new generation of computer printers are truly amazing."

Paul grinned. "All right. We won't worry about the invitations then. The details can wait a bit." He looked to Cassidy. "Now, three hundred costumes, how big a problem is that?"

She bent her head over the computer printout spread across the countertop, distinctly aware of Paul's proximity and William's silent discomfort. "Not too much," she mumbled, "providing I don't take any more New Year's reservations."

Paul frowned and leaned forward, craning his neck to bring his head close to hers. "I don't want you to pass up business."

"Well," she said, straightening to put a bit of distance between them, "I could take a few racks on consignment, maybe. The problem is, I'd have to take what I could get, and chances are it would all be of a theme, something ordered for a play, a period piece."

"Period piece," Paul mused.

Cassidy nodded, and suddenly she had it, the solution to their problems. She clapped her hands together. "That's it!"

Paul looked up, while William lurched forward in concern. She could almost read his thoughts. What goofy thing was his sister about to propose now and into how much trouble was it going to get him? How appalled he would be to discover her feelings for Paul. She tried to concentrate on the issue at hand. "What we need," she said, "is a theme of our own."

Paul rested on one elbow and thought about it. "You could

ake a consignment of costumes in the theme we choose. That would take out a lot of the guesswork, wouldn't it?"

"That's right, and it would simplify matters of decoration, oo. Think about it, a Roman courtyard or…an Old West saoon, maybe."

"I like that," Paul said. "But what kind of space would omething like that require, and where are we going to find it n such short notice?"

William spoke up, apparently as much to his own surprise s anyone's. "What about the old factory?"

Paul's gaze snapped around. Cassidy watched the idea grow n him. "You know, that's not such a bad idea." He looked t Cassidy, explaining, "We're going to tear it down to make vay for a new state-of-the-art distribution center, but not beause the building is unsound. It's old, and frankly it's ugly, ut it's huge and empty and safe."

Cassidy shrugged. "Sounds good to me, but shouldn't you heck it out with Betina?"

Paul tapped his chin with a forefinger, thinking. "Let's nail own this theme thing, first. Ideas anyone?"

After several minutes of brainstorming, William suggested aat it ought to be something to do with the business, and uddenly Cassidy felt the brush of inspiration again. "Paul, ho founded Barclay Bakeries?"

"My great-grandfather, in 1902. Why?"

"Because it makes sense to go back to the beginning, oesn't it?"

"Back to the beginning?" William echoed. "But our new ocus is the future. You've said so, countless times yourself, aul. Five years from now, Barclay will be not only the preominant local and regional producer of fine wholesale baked oods but the *national* leader as well. Isn't that the point?"

"You're absolutely right, Will," Paul mused. "Barclay is ised on the brink of a whole new era." He turned a look of profound respect on Cassidy, saying, "What better time to look back at our beginnings? Dallas, 1902."

"You know," Cassidy said, excitement ringing through her voice, "I'll bet we could hire some students from the university art and drama departments to help us develop decorative sets. Do you have any old pictures of the business?"

"Do I! The office halls are lined with them."

"We might even make more use of those drama students," she murmured, thinking that she had to talk to Tony—and start looking for period costumes and organize theme development and make lists of everything and— No, those were Betina's jobs.

"Wouldn't it be good," William said tentatively, "if we could somehow tell the story of the development of Barclay Bakeries? How we started, how we've grown, where we're going..."

Cassidy's eyes grew wide. "Oh, my goodness! We could do a little play." She pointed at Paul. "You could be your great-grandfather."

Paul's face was animated. She could see the ideas flickering behind the light in his eyes. Suddenly he leaned forward, seized her head in both hands and dragged her toward him to kiss her hard on the mouth. "You're brilliant!"

Despite the thrill of spontaneous affection, Cassidy felt William's shock and disapproval like a wave of cold air. She smiled at Paul but cut her eyes sideways slightly. She saw understanding flash in Paul's eyes the instant before he turned his bight smile on William. "You're both brilliant!" he exclaimed, throwing an arm around William's neck in a kind of combination hug and hammerlock. "The brilliant Pennos!" Paul laughed, but Cassidy caught the worry that flickered across her brother's face before he gave in to the smile expected of him, and she had to wonder just how ill that boded for her. But then, how much worse did it get than a broken heart, and what else, really, could she expect in the end?

* * *

She got part of her answer the next evening when William showed up at her house, agitated and sharp-tongued. "This is all your fault!" he told her. "You're going to cost me my job, I know it!"

"What are you talking about?"

"The idea is to bring Paul and Betina closer together, not drive a wedge between them!"

Cassidy closed her eyes and took a deep breath before urging William into the low armchair in her small living room. It was purple brocade, and he had long ago proclaimed it hideous, but it was the most comfortable seat in the house. Sitting on the end of the imaginatively draped and fringed sofa, she switched on the Tiffany-style table lamp. "Now tell me what's happened."

Sunshine came into the room and rubbed herself against William's ankle. He gave her a nervous kick that sent her leaping into Cassidy's lap. "It's Paul," he said miserably. "He's paying more attention to this ball than he is to Betina, and she's dumped the decorations on him in retaliation!"

Cassidy sat back and folded her arms, Sunshine curling up in her lap. "How is that my fault?"

William sent her a hard look. "Don't play coy with me, Cassidy Jane Penno. I don't know how you've done it, but you've given Paul...ideas."

Cassidy rolled her eyes. "The only ideas I've given Paul are the kind he's paying me for. I do have some expertise, you know."

"In costumes!" he exclaimed. "You don't know anything about balls!"

"I know about theme and decor and staging. I can help with this. Paul knows it, why don't you?"

"There's something strange going on here, Cassidy! Paul shouldn't know you as well as he seems to!"

Cassidy looked away. "Don't be absurd. We've already worked together once. Of course he *knows* me."

"But he seems to *like* you."

Her mouth fell open. "Is that such a shock? Can't you imagine anyone liking your dopey little sister?"

William had the good grace to look ashamed for a moment. "I didn't mean it like that."

"For your information, William, lots of people like me."

"But Paul's confidence in you developed so quickly!" he argued.

She shrugged, trying for nonchalance. "We just hit it off, that's all."

He studied her for a long moment. She could feel his light green eyes boring holes into her head. He slid to the edge of the chair and said earnestly, "He's taken, Cassidy. You understand that, don't you?"

Startled, she may have given away a little more than she intended. "Not yet."

Alarm sent William to his feet. "You can't honestly think that you have a chance with him!"

She felt the color drain from her face. "I didn't say that."

William went down into a crouch in front of her. "Listen to me, Cassidy," he said in the voice that she recognized as his caring-big-brother tone. "You can't compete with Betina Lincoln. She's a sophisticated, savvy woman, a tall, willowy blonde built to make a man's mouth water. And she knows how to use what she's got to her best advantage. She'll never let you—or any other woman—take Paul away from her."

Cassidy wanted to tell him that Betina Lincoln didn't have Paul...yet. She wanted to say that Paul Spencer was already half in love with her, Cassidy Penno. But she knew that, ultimately, William was right. She was just a friendly face who had appeared at the right time amid the chaos of Paul's life. In the end he would marry Betina because he had to, because he was expected to, and probably because deep down, his pride aside, he really wanted to. Cassidy ignored the pain she felt. She had learned how so long ago that it was almost automatic, as was the reassurance she sought to give her brother. That, too, she had learned to do. It was her chief role in the family, giving reassurance, accepting criticism and disappointment, disseminating the collective unease. She put a hand to her hair and smiled with manufactured amusement.

"For heaven's sake, William, you can't think I'd pit myself against a woman like Betina Lincoln! All I'm trying to do is make a living. It's the same with you."

Some of the worry lines eased out of his forehead. "You're quite right. My livelihood is tied to Paul Spencer in no uncertain terms."

"Exactly," she said, lifting her hands in innocent agreement. "Paul Spencer is a source of income for both of us, only temporarily for me, of course. But as a small business woman, I have to take income where I find it, you know. And I have you to thank for sending Paul Spencer to me."

William's gaze turned inward pensively. "Hmm, I suppose it could work out for the best, properly handled."

"And just think," she added persuasively, "how grateful Paul's bound to be when *your* connections provide him the solutions to his problems."

William's eyes narrowed as if he were gauging Paul's gratitude in advance. "It could happen. Just remember that we can't afford to alienate Betina in the process."

We? Cassidy thought, but she kept her mouth closed and her expression neutral. William pushed up to his full height and stroked his chin in thought. Finally he turned his attention down to Cassidy. "What we have to do, sister dear, is find a way to make Betina the star of the evening."

Cassidy squelched a flash of resentment and nodded obediently. The last thing she wanted to do was shine a spotlight on Betina Lincoln, but if it was necessary to put William's fears to rest—and if it made Paul's life easier in the bargain... She lifted her chin, unaware that she was rising yet again to meet another of the challenges so often set for her by her family—at her own expense. As usual.

William's face took on a cagey look. "Do you know," he said, "I think we should try our hand at writing a play, you and I. Yes, yes, I think that's the ticket." He popped down on the sofa next to Cassidy and smiled in a supremely self-satisfied way. "I happen to know quite a lot about the history of Barclay Bakeries, you know, and with your knowledge of the theater, we ought to be able to craft a sufficiently impressive piece."

"Don't you think Paul ought to make these decisions?" Cassidy asked.

"He's already given the idea his endorsement," Paul pointed out. "The person we really have to please is Betina."

"And how do you propose we do that?"

He leaned forward eagerly. "It's very simple, really. We write the part of Paul's great-grandmother with Betina in mind, you know, the classic woman behind the great man." He paused thoughtfully, eyes narrowing. "Actually, it wouldn't be stretching the truth. I mean, they were a team, you know. He was the creative genius. They were his recipes, after all, but she was a baker, too, and she believed in him totally. I'm told that she worked by his side every step of the way."

Did Betina believe in Paul? Cassidy wondered. She ought to. Given the complete control that he deserved, Paul would undoubtedly lead Barclay Bakeries to the number one spot in the nation. He deserved the chance to prove himself, and apparently only marriage to Betina Lincoln would give him that chance. She didn't stop to think that it was not, strictly speaking, up to her to see to it that Paul got his chance. She only knew, instinctively, that she was going to do everything possible to make it happen. The wheels of her mind were already turning.

"You know, given the time restraints, simpler is better in

this case. We need to do as much as we can through narration. That way, the actors don't have to learn lines, not too many, anyway.''

"You mean they'll be pantomiming."

"Something like that."

"Yes, I see the wisdom there."

"Good. Now we need all the details. You know the story, so let's hear it."

William scratched his head and began speaking. Minutes later, Cassidy got up to fetch paper and pen, and they moved into the kitchen, making use of the table there. Two hours later they picked up the phone and called Tony Abatto. Tony and pizzas arrived a half hour later, and shortly after that a friend of Tony's came—a friend with a deep, resonant voice and a relaxed but expressive way of reading drama aloud.

Cassidy did not realize to what extent she had taken on the dual role of director and producer, but a look traded between Tony and William clearly demonstrated their mutual notice and surprise. As for Tony's friend with ''The Voice,'' he never questioned Cassidy's ability or authority, she so obviously knew what she was doing.

Cassidy went to bed late that night, exhausted but satisfied. Thoughts and ideas continued to percolate through her mind, however: scenes, sets, costumes, lighting... She saw with her mind's eye Paul, dressed for the turn-of-the-century, working industriously in the old-fashioned kitchen of his home, wife at his side, her long skirts swaying gracefully as she moved, her long hair pinned loosely atop her head. Her eyes shone with love and confidence. Paul stopped what he was doing to put his arms around her and hold her close as the narrator extolled her limitless support as the premier factor in the formation and success of the original Barclay Bakery. The face of that loving, supportive woman was not that of Betina Lincoln, and not merely because Cassidy had never seen the woman. No, the face of the woman in Paul's arms was Cassidy's own, because in her heart that was where she wanted to be.

Yet in her heart Cassidy did not, could not, believe that she could or should be the woman to truly hold Paul Spencer. No, that role must ultimately belong to someone more beautiful, more intelligent, more worthy than she. Apparently, at least according to William, that woman was Betina Lincoln, and Cassidy couldn't help thinking that once she and Paul were married, his feelings toward Betina would change. How could he not come to love such a strong, determined woman, a woman to "make a man's mouth water," as William put it. She couldn't hope to compete with such a woman herself. No, she would be happy just being more than friends with Paul, just a little more than friends. It was enough. It would have to be enough.

Chapter Five

"I have the photographs," William said, producing a manila folder from his briefcase. Cassidy, Tony and a trio of Tony's fellow students looked up from the table that Cassidy had set up in the back of the shop.

"There's one in here of the Barclays' kitchen," he said, digging through the folder.

Cassidy put her hands together in a gesture of prayer. "Thank heavens!"

"Actually, it's a recreation, but the old man himself had it done in the twenties for an advertising campaign. They were opening their third shop."

Cassidy and the others poured over the photos avidly. Paul strode into the room, his phone held to the side of his head, movements jerky, face radiating anger and frustration. "That's the most inane thing I've ever heard! No one's trying—" He broke off, ground his teeth and slapped the phone shut before dropping it into his coat pocket. He looked around at the faces now staring at him and growled, "Someone better get to minding the shop. There are customers out front!"

Tony gasped, straightened, and hurried away. Paul glanced at Cassidy and thrust a hand through his hair, muttering, "I never should have gotten you into this. Your business is falling apart, and you're sitting around here agonizing over plans for someone else to tear apart!"

The students traded looks and developed sudden needs to be elsewhere. William sat down in one of their vacant folding chairs and moaned softly, his face woebegone, a hand clamped over his mouth. Cassidy sent worried looks from Paul to him and back to Paul, who jingled change in his pocket and muttered unintelligibly. Finally William ventured pitifully, "She didn't like the script?"

Cassidy's heart sank. They'd worked so hard on that script, their number-one purpose being, other than telling the Barclay story, to give Betina an important central role as Paul's great-grandmother. How were they going to manage a rewrite with time running so short? Paul sighed and pinched the bridge of his nose. "She says that playing the part of my great-grandmother will ruin her image."

"Ruin her image?" Cassidy echoed in confusion. "But your great-grandmother was central to the development of the company!"

"Yes, she was, and for many years!" William exclaimed, sounding as confused as Cassidy.

Paul stabbed a finger in William's direction. "Exactly! The old girl lived years longer than great-grandfather."

"Didn't she die in like 1975?" Cassidy asked.

"At ninety-four," Paul confirmed. "She was the one who lived to see the company become more than a string of bakery shops. Her own son turned Barclay's into a true manufacturer in the modern sense of the word. And that's the problem!"

William shook his head. "I don't understand. I thought Miss Lincoln would be pleased to have such a pivotal role in our little drama."

Paul put his hands to his hips and said coldly, "*Miss* Lincoln, as it turns out, is vain to the point of idiocy! She refuses to play the part of an 'old woman.' Her words.''

"But the role begins with a very young woman, only twenty-one years-old and newly married,'' Cassidy argued.

"That doesn't matter!'' Paul exclaimed, throwing up his hands. "The woman ages, and Betina believes that will ruin her image with all those people who'll be in attendance. She even says the makeup to create the illusion of an older woman will ruin her skin!''

Cassidy stared a moment at Paul, sure she'd missed something important along the way somewhere. No woman could be *that* vain. Could she? Hopefully, she looked to her brother for explanation. William's mouth was hanging open, alerting Cassidy that she, too, was gaping. She snapped her mouth shut with an audible click. William, too, struggled for composure.

"I-I'm s-sure Miss Lincoln m-misunderstands the, um, significance of the role,'' he sputtered. "You're off stage after the first two scenes, while she remains an important figure almost throughout.''

"Doesn't matter,'' Paul said succinctly. "She won't appear as an older woman, period.'' He lifted his face to the ceiling and exclaimed, "God, that woman makes me want to contemplate murder instead of matrimony!''

William was near tears. "What are we to do?'' he wailed.

Paul struck a pose, hands on hips, head bowed, eyes riveted on Cassidy. "We'll just have to find someone else to play the part,'' he said, "and I know just the lady to do us proud.''

Cassidy and William gasped in unison. William, as usual, found his voice first. "Y-you can't mean—''

"Oh, Paul, no. I don't dare!''

Paul grabbed the back of the chair next to her and dragged it close, dropping down onto the edge of its seat. "It's either that or can the whole idea, Cass,'' he said urgently, finding her hands with his. "Listen, babe, I know I've pushed friendship to its very limits where we're concerned, but there's no one else to do this, no one else I want to do it with. I'll make it worth your while, I promise.''

"Oh, Paul, no! It's not a matter of money..."

"I know that," he said quickly, his voice going all silky and soft, "but I don't have any other way to reward you for your support and your generosity...and your sweetness." He reached up and stroked her cheek with the backs of the fingers of one hand. Cassidy melted, even knowing it was stupid.

William groaned and slid down in his chair, wailing, "Oh, no!''

Paul yanked his hand away and turned a glare on William.

"Sir," William pleaded, "Paul, I beg you. Think what you're doing!"

"What else can I do?" Paul demanded.

"But Miss Lincoln—"

"*Miss* Lincoln knows perfectly well that I have to find someone else to play the part. I warned her that I would, and she insisted that I do so!'' Paul looked again to Cassidy, whose doubts must still have shown on her face, for he turned at once to William and demanded, "Tell her to do it!''

"Me?" William protested.

"You're the one whose disapproval she worries about," Paul pointed out.

William sat up in his chair, his gaze going to Cassidy. A look of some cagey force came over him, straightening his spine, lifting his chin, narrowing and hardening his eyes. "Well, by all means, then," he said smoothly. Leaning forward, he pinned Cass with a look that frankly displayed a certain power. Cassidy shivered with the sudden knowledge that William would always wield that certain power over her— if she allowed him to. "We can't let Paul down," he was saying.

She wondered if supporting Paul was as important to him as he made it sound, and in the next heartbeat discarded the question as irrelevant. She turned her attention to Paul himself, sure of what she must do and why. "Of course, I'll play the part, if that's what you want."

Relief slumped Paul in his chair. "Thank you. Thank you, Cassidy."

William asserted himself again, saying, "We'll need to make some revisions, of course, in the early part of the script, but that—"

"No revisions," Paul stated flatly, daring William with a look to so much as argue.

William swallowed whatever he'd been about to say, and Cassidy pulled her hands from Paul's, disciplining the small flare of satisfaction that William's sudden loss of aggression produced. Subtly, she took control of the moment, pulling William's folder of photos toward her. "Now let's see what we can find of use here."

Actually, they found a great deal of use, and within the hour Cassidy was out scouring antique and junk shops for the furnishings she needed. Paul had given her his flip phone, so that she could call when she found something she wanted to buy and he could arrange payment and delivery. By the time she returned to the costume shop at the end of the day, she felt that she'd moved mountains and was excited about a new idea concerning the decorations. She couldn't wait to speak to Paul about it. She barely heard Tony's goodbye as he hurried away, she was so busy dialing up Paul for the umpteenth time. The call hadn't even gone through, however, when Paul himself opened the door and walked into the shop. She slapped the phone together and thrust it at him.

"Oh, Paul, I have the most wonderful idea!"

"Great!" he said, dropping the phone into his pocket and taking her by the arm. "Tell me all about it over dinner."

She barely registered his words, so caught up was she with her idea. "It's that picture of your great-grandmother's kitchen," she said excitedly, "and the way Hoot has decorated the restaurant. Think of it! We'll decorate all the dining tables at the ball the same way your great-grandmother decorated hers!''

''Marvelous!'' he said, maneuvering her around the shop as he flicked off lights and set the alarm.

''I'm hoping that Hoot can tell us where he got all that old mismatched flatware and—''

''Oh, I'm sure Hoot can do better than that,'' he said, grinning at her. ''Maybe he'll loan it to us.'

''Do you think so? What about his tables and chairs? Do you think there's a chance?''

Paul laughed and shoved her out the door, pulling her coat together and buttoning it. ''Give me your keys.''

''What?''

''Your keys, silly, so I can lock the door.''

''Oh, my goodness! Tony—''

''Tony is gone,'' he assured her. ''Now it's our turn.'' He snapped his fingers together twice. ''Keys, if you please.''

Laughing, she dug them out of her purse and dropped them into his hand, saying, ''I can't believe how everything's falling into place.''

''I can,'' he said, glancing back over his shoulder at her as he fitted the key into the first lock.

She was already on to another subject. ''We're going to need a couple of bolts of gingham to make tablecloths like your grandmother's, and those little cream pitchers for the flowers will have to be ordered. A man showed me a wholesaler's catalog of reproductions, today. I think we can work a deal, but I wanted to run everything by you first. Anyway, I told him—''

Paul stopped and hauled her around to face him. She hadn't even realized they were walking!

''What?''

''This,'' he said, pulling her to him. His mouth covered hers and stayed there for a long time, gently plying and manipulating until every other thought but kissing him back had left her head. She looped her arms around his neck and simply gave herself up to it, knowing somehow that this was part and parcel of the tacit agreement they'd made when they'd begun to work together. They couldn't be together without this, not for long, and she wouldn't think now of the time when they could not be together at all— because of this. It didn't matter. Nothing and no one mattered except Paul. She understood that suddenly with such awful clarity and equal acceptance. She wouldn't say that she was sorry, not even to herself, because somehow she knew that this was right. She and Paul Spencer together, as incredible as it seemed, was right.

Fate conspired to rob them both, and Fate would undoubtedly win, but not yet, not until after the ball. They deserved that much. *She* deserved that much, and she surprised herself by determining, somehow, to have it. That determination finally broke the kiss as she pulled her mouth from his, and, fixing her hands around the lapels of his coat, she looked up at him.

"Don't ask her again until the new year," she said softly. "Please. Give us that much time. Don't ask her until January."

"All right," he said. "I promise."

She laid her head against his shoulder and closed her eyes, letting him hold her, warming her against the cool evening air.

"We make a good team," he told her wistfully, and she smiled into the front of his coat.

"A very good team."

Until January. Only until January.

It was utter chaos in the beginning. The factory was dusty and chilly, the lighting too harsh and glaring. Tony and the half dozen recruits he'd managed to find for them were running around like the kids they were, playing an imaginary game of basketball without benefit of equipment. Paul came in late, while William and Cassidy were arguing about what should go where, and promptly got on the phone, demanding to know why the place hadn't been cleaned as he'd ordered. Cassidy realized that their first practice was accomplishing less than nothing and understood with some dismay that only she could whip things into shape.

Leaving William talking to himself, she strode to the middle of the cavernous space and called for attention. When she didn't get it, she waved her arms over her head and tried again. Finally she put her fingers in her mouth and let loose a deafening whistle. Everyone else immediately stopped what they were doing and turned in her direction, William with his mouth hanging open as if he couldn't quite believe she'd called such attention to herself. Paul recovered from his surprise first, spoke briefly into the phone and put it away, his attention riveted.

Cassidy smiled slightly at his show of deference and lifted her chin, pitching her voice to carry clearly. "Thank you for coming. I'm sure you'll agree that the sooner we begin, the sooner we may all go home." General murmurs of agreement followed. She acknowledged them with a nod of her head and lifted a hand in Paul's direction. "Paul, perhaps you have something to say to us?"

He nodded, cleared his throat, and wandered closer. "Thank you for coming on such short notice. I suppose the matter we must first address is the scheduling of subsequent rehearsals. What times would you say are best?"

A discussion followed, concerning late evenings versus early mornings. Late evenings proved most convenient. Mondays, Wednesdays and Thursdays were settled on as the most workable days. With those matters settled, Paul turned the discussion to that of roles. "I will play the part of the late Theo Barclay myself, and Miss Penno—"

"Cassidy," she corrected.

"Thank you. Cassidy will play the part of my wife, er, Theo Barclay's wife, my great-grandmother, actually. That is,

Jane." Some laughter followed that bumbling remark, but Paul received it good-naturedly. He went on. "She is, also, the creative intelligence beyond the power, which—frankly— would be me." More laughter. "That being the case, you may take her word as you would mine. In other words, do just what she tells you." Tony lifted a brow at that. William lifted two, but no one else batted so much as an eyelash.

Paul deferred to Cassidy, who began by passing out scripts. She introduced the narrator as Andy, saying that other parts— most notably those of Paul's grandfather, both as a boy and a man, and various other family members and business associates, and of course Paul himself, again as both boy and man— were up for grabs. Tony made the suggestion that Paul play his adult self as well as his own great-grandfather, and Cassidy agreed that such casting would lend the production the satisfying feeling of a circle completed. Paul readily accepted that added responsibility, and the subject of youngsters to play the young Theo and Paul came up. William stepped in here.

"I've been thinking about that. Why don't we invite the children of our executive staff at Barclay to try out for those parts? They'd have to be of a certain age, of course, and boys, naturally, but there ought to be one or two with some acting ability and the desire to show it off."

"A very good idea," Paul replied. "The Pennos ride to the rescue again. I'll leave the wording and dissemination of said casting call to you, Will, if that's all right."

William preened self-importantly. "Of course."

"It wouldn't hurt to have a girl or two in the background," Cassidy said.

"I'll see to it," William promised.

That settled, Cassidy called Paul and William aside and put everyone else to reading over the script. To Paul she explained the dilemma that she and William had been so ardently discussing during his arrival. "William thinks a theater in the round approach would be most interesting, but as a ball includes dancing, and dancing requires a good deal of room, I wonder if it wouldn't be better to stage the drama against the far wall there.''

Paul studied the enormous room, wondering aloud how the caterer could most easily enter and exit and where the orchestra that Betina had hired would best be placed. After only a few minutes of discussion, he decided that Cassie's idea was most easily workable. A stage would be built against the far wall, with tables and chairs set up before it. The dance floor would be laid on the other side of the tables and chairs, with the orchestra pit built against the opposite wall. The caterer could set up buffet lines at either end.

Betina had said something about draping the entire interior of the building in white, but Paul wondered aloud if circus stripes or an old-fashioned county fair look might not be more in keeping with their theme. William argued vociferously for Betina's vision in white, but Cassidy agreed with Paul that stripes or bright blocks of color would be more in keeping with their turn-of-the-century theme. William feared that it might not be politic to deny Betina her preference, to which argument Paul snapped, "I might have to marry the woman, but I don't have to indulge her every whim! Everyone might as well understand that now!''

William looked shocked, but then he turned a fulminating stare on Cassidy, as if he blamed *her* for Paul's attitude. Cassidy felt both uncomfortable and unfairly persecuted. It wasn't her fault that Paul could not seem to get along with Betina. She wished suddenly that Paul hadn't fallen in so completely with her ideas. William was already suspicious. She remembered the kiss they'd shared on the sidewalk outside her shop only days earlier, and imagined what might have happened if William had come upon them during that time. She shuddered to think what he might have said or done. She had no doubt that she would have caught the brunt of it.

Pushing such unpleasant thoughts out of mind, Cassidy suggested that they get on to assigning parts for the drama. As the script contained few spoken lines, the issue of who should play whom became more one of type and appearance than acting ability. The roles, therefore, were relatively easy to assign, which led rather quickly to a confusing discussion of staging. Paul called a halt by announcing firmly that Cassidy would decide such issues and inform everyone else of them. Period. With that all eyes turned to her.

Self-consciously, Cassidy set about directing the setup of an approximation of the first scene, that of Paul's great-grandparents' kitchen. Not much guesswork was involved here as they had the photo to guide them. So, using an old metal table, some boxes and a three-legged desk, they quickly set up a practice space. Cassidy herself read the direction she and William had written out by hand and his secretary had typed. Then she relinquished her script to William and, together with Paul, set about fitting action to narration.

It was laughably easy. Andy quickly picked up on the right pacing and elocution to make the narration work, and as for Paul and Cassidy, they might have been thinking with one mind, so completely did their actions, mannerisms and expressions mesh. When Andy spoke about the newlywed Barclays' decision to quit their jobs—he as a baker, she as a pastry glazer—in order to sell baked goods based on Theo's own recipes out of their own kitchen, the script called for "Jane" and "Theo" to clasp hands and look into each other's eyes. Paul and Cassidy did that, but then Paul quite naturally reached out and slipped his arm about Cassidy's shoulders, pulling her to him in a gesture of reassurance, creating a particularly poignant moment. Those watching applauded, everyone but William, who tried to hide his frown with a prolonged study of the script. All too aware of William's displeasure and the raptness of their audience, Cassidy quickly pulled away, but physical distance did little to still the pounding of her heart or dull the sharpness of her yearning for a reality based upon what was pure pretense.

Thankfully, Tony provided distraction. Putting his head together with that of another student, he had come up with an idea for staging that was both workable and efficient. After much discussion and description, they devised a plan for three separate sets, each accommodating two scenes with only minor changes. To save themselves the expense and difficulty of constructing a massive curtain, they hit upon the idea of building the sets behind scrims, which would then be backlit and essentially rendered invisible. Tony even promised to look into the possibility of borrowing the fabric screens from the university.

All in all, it was a productive first "rehearsal," and everyone left encouraged. But when Paul quietly urged Cassidy to allow him to take her for coffee or even a late supper, she felt that she had to decline, as it was evident to her that William was hanging around to ensure that just such a thing did not happen. Paul whispered that he'd call her later, brushed a kiss across her cheek and handed her into her car with a reluctant smile.

William sauntered over to speak to Cassidy, blatantly making certain that she was going straight home...alone. Cassidy did just that, and along the way, puttering patiently in her little car, she made an unsurprising discovery about herself. She wasn't cut out for conducting clandestine affairs, however innocent, and neither, apparently, was Paul. She accepted the depressing conclusion that her relationship with Paul would have to be redefined, and she was determined to broach the subject openly when he called.

But Paul did not call. Instead he showed up around ten o'clock, agitated and nervous, his hair still wet from a recent shower. He was wearing dark, relaxed-fit jeans, white leather athletic shoes, and a bloodred T-shirt beneath a blue plaid flannel shirt, which had been left unbuttoned with the ta hanging out. He came right in, took a seat in the center of her couch and said, "We have to talk."

"Yes, I agree," she told him, dropping down into the arm chair. Before she could say more, he was off and running with an amazing proclamation.

"I'm sorry, Cass, but I'm just not hypocrite enough to pretend that I'm not crazy about you. I'm still a free man, and as long as I am, I want to be with you."

Cassidy was momentarily dumbfounded, but at length she found the presence of mind to ask, "Paul, is that really possible? What about Betina? Won't she be offended if you're seen too often in my company?"

He pushed both hands over his face and hair, saying, "I don't know, Cass. I don't honestly care."

She didn't know what to say to that, for it didn't really change anything if she understood the problem correctly. Perhaps that was where she ought to start, understanding the problem. She screwed up her courage and said, "Paul, do you really have to marry her?"

For a long, agonizing moment, Paul said nothing, merely sat and stared at his hands. And then, quite strongly, he said, "Yes."

Disappointment came like a blow to Cassidy. She bit her lip and looked away, seeking to disguise the tears gathering in her eyes.

Paul sighed deeply. "I just can't see any other way. She has the upper hand, and she's made it plain what she wants. The only way that I can secure the business and ensure the entire family's income is to give her what she wants, though why she'd want to be married to me when she knows how I feel about her, I can't begin to understand."

Cassidy smiled wistfully. "I know you believe that being a legitimate part of the family is driving this obsession of hers, but Paul, I can't help thinking that she has to be in love with you."

He shook his head. "That's because you could never understand a person like her. Cass, I don't honestly think Betina is capable of loving anyone, not even herself."

Cassidy shuddered. She contemplated a long time before asking her next question. "I don't suppose she'll settle for a marriage in name only?"

"She'll have to," he said darkly. "She's quite confident that she can change my mind once we're legally married, but I have to tell you that I cannot imagine making love to that...that soulless, calculating—"

But you did before! Cassidy found herself thinking. She felt a surprising amount of resentment about it, too—as if she had any right! She took a deep breath, steeling herself for what she had to say next. "Paul, you have to know that my brother is very disturbed by our...involvement. I don't—"

"Your brother," he interrupted hotly, "had best watch his step around me. I don't like the way he browbeats you! What right does he have to judge you, anyway?"

Cassidy was touched by his defense of her. She was a little miffed with William herself, but she wasn't exactly conducting herself in an inspiringly sensible manner just now. She smiled wanly and inclined her head. "Does your family hold no claim on your behavior and consideration then, Paul?"

He quite visibly blanched. After a protracted silence, he answered miserably. "You know they do."

She knew all too well, of course. She looked away, blinking back tears. "I just don't see any way that we can really be together, Paul, not even for a short while."

He slid right to the edge of the couch and leaned toward her, capturing her gaze and holding it intently. "Sweetheart, just the other day you asked me not to allow myself to become engaged to Betina until after New Year's. Are you saying now that you've changed your mind about that?"

Cassidy stared in dismay. If she said that she had changed her mind, would he go out and fix it with Betina? She couldn't quite bear the thought. And yet, neither of them were very good at pretending to be casual friends. What should she say then? Quite without meaning to, she shook her head, and he took that as the truth that it was. He came right off the couch and knelt before her, his large, strong hands covering her knees.

"Do you still mean to help me with the ball?"

She was a bit startled by the idea that he would think she might abandon him when he so obviously needed her. "Of course!"

It was obviously the answer that he expected. "Then we'll be together at times."

"Yes. So?"

"Cass, I can't be with you without being happy about it," he said. "Touching you is the most natural thing I've ever done. I can't seem not to. When you're near I have the most wonderful feeling that all is well, that life is good. When I walk into your shop or your home or even a great, ugly barn of a building and find you there, it becomes the most comfortable, welcoming place I can think of. I can't seem to hide those feelings, and I don't want to. But I don't want to hurt you, either. I don't want to embarrass or shame you—"

"Oh, no, Paul, don't ever think that! I am not ashamed. I've done nothing to be ashamed of and neither have you. It's only that…William has never understood me."

"William's an idiot."

"William has his faults," she qualified, "but he's not an idiot. He knows we're…something more than friends. It must seem terribly foolish to him, and he's obviously concerned for both of us."

"And himself, no doubt," Paul added cryptically.

She wouldn't bother confirming that assertion. It didn't seem to matter what William thought, anyway. Nothing seemed to matter but Paul. God help her. "Don't worry about William," she said. "I've dealt with William all my life."

He reached up and stroked her cheek, making no promises, but then she expected none. "Where does that leave us then, Cass?"

She shook her head, but she was smiling. She felt the most wonderful helplessness. "Right here, I suppose," she said.

He laid his palm alongside her face and tilted his head. "I'm sorry, love."

"For what?"

He sighed. "For finding you when it was too late. For being so stupid as to let myself be trapped by my stepcousin. For not being able to control my feelings somehow."

She laughed at that, very lightly, almost soundlessly. "The timing and the feelings belong to both of us," she pointed out, "and you are trapped because you are an honorable man who will not shirk his responsibilities. I don't see reason for apology in that."

"You wouldn't," he whispered, "not my Cassidy."

His Cassidy. She wasn't, of course, and yet paradoxically she was. She turned her head slightly and kissed his palm. Sighing, he closed his eyes and sank down, laying his head on her lap. She stroked his temple with her fingertips. Slowly but deliberately his hand skimmed downward and came to rest against her breast, fingers spreading wide to encompass it. He turned his face into her lap and slid his other hand up the outside of her thigh.

She put her head back and closed her eyes, her heart thudding with such force that each beat seemed to reverberate along every nerve ending, and yet she felt an almost paralyzing languor. For a long while, they stayed just as they were. And then his hand seemed to convulse and tighten over her breast. A streak of desire as hot as lightning flashed through her.

He lifted his head, straightened and removed his hand in one fluid movement. Sitting back on his heels, he said, "I'd better go."

She nodded, knowing that if he stayed they ran the risk of

giving in to desires better left unexplored under the circumstances. Yet nodding, rising, and following him to the door were the most difficult operations she had ever executed. She felt as though she were wading through chest-deep water. He paused in the open doorway and glanced over his shoulder, then turned to face her.

"Have I told you that I love this room?"

She followed his gaze with her own, looking around at the cranberry red walls and gold moldings, the fringe on the valances and throw pillows, the purples and maroons in the eclectic patterns of the furnishings, the moss green background in the ornately patterned rug. She smiled. "No, I don't think you have."

"It's so warm, passionate, almost decadent...and imaginative. Unique. Very *you*."

She laughed at that. He leaned forward and kissed her lightly on the mouth.

"Bye."

She watched him all the way down the walk to his car, then lifted her hand and returned his wave before closing the door and locking it. She switched off the light and wandered blindly into the hall, where a nightlight in the shape of a Cupid with drawn bow lit the doorway to her bedroom. Sunshine lay on a rug just inside the door, snoozing peacefully. Cassidy bent and scratched her head until the cat stretched and yawned and allowed herself to be scooped up.

"Sorry, chum," Cassidy told her, "but I feel the need of a little company." She scratched the cat beneath the chin, murmuring softly, "And I always will. I'm very much afraid that I always will."

Chapter Six

She ran from the parking lot, squeezed through the opening someone had made by rolling back the heavy corrugated metal door on the side of the factory and was greeted by exclamations of relief. Paul hurried forward to receive her. "Thank God!" He threw an arm about her shoulders and ushered her into the center of the group. "I was worried about you. It isn't like you to be late."

"You've kept everyone waiting!" William snapped, frowning at the way Paul kept his arm draped about her.

She sidled away from Paul. "Sorry. I had a meeting with a wig salesman, and it took longer than I'd planned. Then there was a wreck on Central."

"You should have known better than to come up Central," William scolded.

Paul quickened, his hands going to his waist. "What's your problem, Penno? Just get off her back."

Cassidy laid a calming hand on his upper arm, saying, "Let's not spend any more time on this. We have work to do."

Paul relaxed his posture and stepped back. William frowned and said nothing, his gaze troubled. Cassidy felt a flash of sympathy for her poor brother. No doubt he felt himself very betrayed by his foolish baby sister, but despite nights and days of anxious, confused, even prayerful study, she could find no way to relieve either William's fears or her own. Facts were facts. She was in love with a man who would shortly marry someone else and be forever out of her reach. Given that unchangeable future, she would be wise to end her association with Paul now. But she couldn't do it. She simply could not walk away from him now, and she could only hope that she would find the strength necessary to do so in the future. Otherwise, poor William was going to find himself brother to a married man's mistress.

Every time the phrase materialized in her mind, she felt the shock of it again, and she knew that it was a possibility she had been considering, if only subconsciously. It seemed to her the saddest thing imaginable—until she imagined a future completely devoid of Paul Barclay Spencer. She simply couldn't think of it anymore, giving herself over gratefully to the more urgent matters at hand.

With a cool efficiency born of sheer relief and utter necessity, she swiftly organized the practice and put it into motion. All went smoothly, despite the many claims on her attention. William demanded final decisions concerning the design and construction of the stages and sets. A petite brunette by the name of Celeste insisted on giving Cassidy a detailed explanation of her lighting designs, while a redhead named Robert made a pitch for plexiglass panels suspended overhead as a means of improving sound quality. Two hours and eighteen minutes after arriving, Cassidy called a halt, pleased with the progress they'd made but mindful of the distance they had left to go.

The group began to break up, some bolting for the door and others lingering to chat among themselves. Only then did Cassidy let up enough to realize that her head had begun pounding, so much so that her first inclination when Tony made a bid for her attention was to head for the door herself. But she worked with Tony, and he was wearing that pouty look of his because she had already put him off a couple times. She smiled and tried to concentrate.

"The thing is," he began, "if we have to style those wigs ourselves, well, we might as well just forget them and style everybody's hair, then we could use the wig money for—"

Cassidy cut him off with a shake of her head, then pressed her fingertips to her scalp in an effort to still the throbbing. "Not all of us have hair the proper length or color and... Can we discuss this later, please?"

"But, Cass—"

"Later," Paul interrupted sternly, reaching between them to clamp a hand around Cassidy's wrist. "What's wrong with you?" he asked her.

"It's nothing. Just a headache."

"She probably hasn't eaten," Tony said, a touch of smugness mixed with the knowledge of familiarity. "She gets these when she doesn't eat."

It was true, Cassidy reflected dimly, that she'd skipped lunch, and breakfast had been a cup of coffee and a piece of toast, but she had so much to do. She sighed, and the top of her head nearly came off. Paul tugged on her wrist.

"I'm taking you to dinner. Come on."

"What she needs is aspirin and a dark room," Tony said.

"She'll get that, too."

Tony grumbled but took himself off. Paul pulled her into the curve of his arm.

"Come on, sweetheart. Let's get you fed and medicated."

Her eyes closed, Cassidy nodded gently and laid her head on his shoulder.

"If Cassidy's ill," William said, "I'd better take her home." It was his don't-bother-arguing-with-me voice, and

Cassidy discovered that she was too tired and in too much pain to do so. Reluctantly she opened her eyes and looked up at Paul apologetically.

"I'm not fit for company tonight," she said.

Paul frowned. "I know you're not. I don't want company. I want to take care of you." Worry roughened his voice and warmed Cassidy from the inside out. She smiled, comforted despite the pounding in her skull. Had she seen the look on William's face, though, she'd have wept.

Stepping into their path as Paul urged her forward again, William said flatly, "I can't allow this to go on any longer."

"Allow?" Paul echoed. "We're all adults here, Will. I don't think it's up to you to *allow* anything."

"Cassidy is my sister."

"Your *grown* sister, and now is not the time for this, not that it's any of your business."

William's tone grew placating. "Paul, please think what you're doing. You're acting as if Cassidy is somehow special to you."

"She is special! Not just to me but to everyone who knows her, except, apparently to her own brother!"

Will chose to ignore this, saying, "Paul, what if Betina should find out—"

"This has nothing to do with Betina!" Paul insisted hotly, pushing past William, his arm holding Cassidy tight to his side. Cassidy moaned and felt tears start behind her eyes.

"Think what you're putting in jeopardy!" William called out. "She's not worth it, Paul!"

Cassidy felt the stillness that came over Paul even before his footsteps halted. He turned to William, folding her against his chest.

"Are you the most insensitive sibling who ever lived or are you just a general idiot?"

Tears leaked from beneath Cassidy's eyelids, the pain in her head somehow blending with the emotional pain of William's obvious disdain. She knew with an objective part of herself that William was right, that the best thing she could do for everyone involved was simply to step away, but the throbbing in her head had increased tenfold in the past few seconds, and the only comfort the whole world seemed to offer was to be found right here in Paul's arms.

She moaned when he stooped and swept her up against him, swiftly carrying her away. She felt the darkness and the cool night air. It seemed both to alleviate somewhat and increase the pounding in her head. The sounds of gravel crunching beneath his feet reverberated from the crown of her skull to the roots of her teeth. He put her into the front seat of his car and belted her in. The closing of the door, gentle as it was, rocked the pain from ear to ear inside her head. He got in beside her and stretched his arm out between the seats.

"You okay?"

"Umm."

"Damn," he said and started up the car engine. "Hang on. I'm taking you home."

They were well on their way when he said gruffly, "Someone needs to take that brother of yours in hand."

"Not you," she managed, thinking of all the difficulties inherent, from Paul being William's boss to the many ways William could make trouble for him.

Paul said nothing more, and in a thankfully short period of time, he was settling her gently onto her own sofa. Sunshine leaped up beside her, purring understandingly. Paul found aspirin and brought them with a glass of water, seeing that she swallowed two before slipping off her shoes and tucking a blanket around her. He left her with a kiss brushed across her forehead and a whispered promise to find them something to eat. Twenty minutes later the pounding inside her skull had relented sufficiently to allow her to sit up. He brought the food in on a cookie sheet, which she received on a pillow placed across her lap.

He had put together a bowl of canned vegetable soup and a small omelet with saltine crackers, a sliced apple and a wedge of dill pickle on the side. As she dived into the soup, she took time to inform him that the large, opaque, plastic container in the refrigerator contained a recently made salad and the fresh dressing was in the shaker bottle in the door. He returned to the kitchen and came back with a "tray" for himself and an extra serving of salad for her. It seemed perfectly natural to have him puttering around in her kitchen, choosing foods for the both of them.

He sat down on the sofa next to her, tossed a kiss at her temple, balanced his tray on his knees and began to eat. Having started first, she finished first. Her head had that airy feeling that comes when the blood vessels constrict in pain then dilate in its aftermath. She leaned back on the cushion and sighed in contentment.

"Feeling better?"

She smiled. "Mmm, much."

"Good. Mind if I turn on the evening news?"

She lifted her head in surprise and looked at the digital clock on the face of the VCR atop the nineteen-inch television in the corner cupboard. Six minutes past ten o'clock! Heavens! Leaning forward, she picked up the remote control from the trunk that served as coffee table, pointed it at the television, and clicked it on. "What channel do you prefer?"

He shrugged, swallowed omelet and said, "This one's fine."

They settled back and watched, one or the other of them commenting on some particular bit at points. During the weather, which promised both sunshine and rain, as well as temperatures in the lower forties, Paul got up and gathered their dishes to carry them into the kitchen. When she started to rise in order to help him, he quickly disabused her of that notion. "Sit yourself down, young lady, and relax. I'm going to stash these in the dishwasher and come right back. You are not to move from this spot."

"Don't be silly. I'm perfectly all right now."

"And you're going to stay that way," he told her.

She rolled her eyes, but she was smiling. She couldn't remember the last time anyone had coddled her. She curled up with Sunshine in her lap to watch a late-night talk show. He returned only a few minutes later, resumed his place beside her, looped an arm about her neck, and pulled her down until her head rested on his shoulder. She squirmed around until she found a comfortable place. He shifted to accommodate her, so that eventually they wound up almost sideways on the couch, her back against his chest, her head resting on his shoulder, his arms curled loosely about her, Sunshine purring contentment for all of them.

As Cassidy drifted deeper into relaxation, her mind touched on the exchange between Paul and William earlier, but she pushed it away, concentrating instead on the almost unbearable sweetness of feeling cherished. Not even sleep could steal it away.

She roused sometime later, dimly aware that she was being carried. She felt the shock of cool sheets beneath her and the tug of her sweater and jeans as he eased her out of them, leaving her clad in camisole, panties, socks, and bra. Then the covers were being tugged up around her chin and smoothed. She hovered at the very brink of unconsciousness, compelled to deeper sleep and yet... Paul bent over her and lightly pressed a kiss to her lips, whispering a good-night, and suddenly she knew what held her back from complete surrender. He was leaving her, and all the comfort would go with him. She fought to lift her arms and turn. It was like moving through heavy syrup in slow motion, but she did manage to mumble, "Don't go. Stay with me."

It seemed that a very long time passed before he replied, "All right, for a while."

A few moments later she sighed as he slipped into bed beside her, his arm tunneling under her neck and folding her against his chest. She was aware that he remained fully dressed, but it didn't matter. He was here. He stayed because he cared. For her. He cared for her. Her arms naturally slid about him, and sleep crept over her, weighing her down with fluffy inertia and blankness.

She woke to sunlight, the certainty that she had overslept, and the feel of a hand, large and warm, against her bare belly. Instinctively she dealt with the hand first, easing away from it, only to become aware of a long arm draped across her body and a solid wall of muscle at her back. Paul. A slow smile stretched across her face, and her body responded in kind, languorously ridding itself of the stiffness of sleep. Paul sighed and rolled closer, his arm tightening as his hand slid lower. Cassidy gasped, sucking in her breath as his fingers slid between her legs. Paul stiffened and went very still, signaling that he was now fully awake.

Cassidy made herself relax and turn onto her side, facing him. She trembled with the effort to ignore his hand. Only when she smiled at him rather sheepishly did he remove it, sliding it up and over her hip. Pulling her closer, he pressed his forehead to hers. She lifted a hand to his cheek, feeling the roughness of his beard.

"Good morning," he said. "How do you feel?"

"Wonderful."

"I can attest to the accuracy of that statement," he said sleepily, his hand roaming over her buttocks and down her leg, then upward again, urging her closer. "You're lovely to wake up to."

"So are you."

He chuckled. "Somehow I doubt that, but let's pretend for the moment that it's true." Rising up slightly, he rolled her onto her back and settled atop her, his upper body weight levered onto his forearms. Nothing, however, not even the layers of clothing between them, prevented her from feeling the weight of rigid male flesh nestled against the apex of her thighs and the flat of her belly. She fought the impulse to spread her legs and bring the contact to an even greater level of intimacy. Then he dropped his head and laid his mouth against hers, his tongue sliding along the seal of her lips. Moaning, she granted him entrance, feeling the plunge of his tongue all the way to the soles of her feet. Her arms came up and wound about him, her body seeming to melt beneath his, and it was as if she went a little mad, her control slipping away as instinct and desire took over.

It was not enough, suddenly. Her back arched, bringing her breasts fully against his chest, her mouth ground against his, their tongues in frantic, sensuous combat. She undulated beneath him, striving to bring every part of her into closer, deeper proximity with him. But still it was not enough. It would never be enough, because no matter how much of him she had, she would always want more. Always. The very idea frightened her suddenly, the certainty that she would forever want what she could not have.

Now as desperate to break contact as she had been a moment before to intensify it, she pressed herself into the mattress and turned her head, ending the kiss. Paul's mouth slid across her cheek to her ear, his teeth nipping at her lobe before attaching themselves to the soft flesh of her neck. She closed her eyes as a fresh wave of desire roared through her. She opened them again—to the sight of her bedside clock. Several moments passed before her mind registered the message that her eyes were sending her, a message Paul needed to hear.

"Dear heaven!"

"Oh, yes," Paul agreed, his breath steaming the flesh that covered her collar bone before his teeth tested it.

"Paul!"

"Hmm?"

"It's nearly 9:00 a.m."

"Mmm. What?"

"I said, it's nearly—"

His head came up and pivoted to the side. "Nine!" he echoed incredulously. "Holy cow!"

Cassidy struggled briefly beneath him, saying, "I have to get up. The shop's supposed to open at ten."

"And I'm supposed to be in the office at eight forty-five," he said wryly.

Cassidy grimaced. "Oops."

He laughed. "You can say that again." But then he sobered, his soft gray eyes boring into hers. "I desperately want to make love to you."

"I know," she answered, warming at the words, "but..."

He nodded, kissed her gently on the mouth and sighed. "I'd better call and let them know I'm going to be late."

"What will you tell them?"

He smiled. "That I slept so well last night I didn't want to leave the bed."

"I'm glad. Thank you for staying with me."

"My pleasure," he whispered, and then he rolled away, tossed aside the covers and rose, fully clothed, to stand in his stocking feet beside the bed. "Do me a favor," he said, bending over her to place a kiss between her eyes.

"What's that?"

"Don't get up until I've gone."

"Why?"

"Because I want to think of you all day long here in this delicious bed—and because I don't think I could resist the sight of you in those little panties and that silky top thing you're wearing."

Her body quickened at his words, but she pulled the covers up to her chin and slid deeper into the bed. "Okay."

He kissed her once again, longingly, on the mouth. Then he picked up his shoes and carried them from the room. She heard the door close softly a few minutes later, and a sense of loss settled over her, forcing out a sigh. The situation was so very ironic. For the first time in her life she had spent the night with a man, and a man whom she loved without any doubt...and still she lay here a virgin. She didn't know whether to be relieved or disappointed. And so she was both.

Cassidy wouldn't have accepted her father's invitation to lunch had she known that her brother would be there, as well. She had neatly avoided William for several days, refusing to take his calls and surrounding herself with other people when she couldn't avoid his presence. His irritation with her was clear from the perpetual glower that he wore on his face and the sharp edge in his voice whenever he spoke, but Cassidy found that she was uninterested in his opinion. He would never understand how she felt about Paul. How could he when she didn't understand it herself? And he certainly did not understand how Paul could feel anything at all for her. Otherwise, he would never have said that she was unworthy of Paul's regard, as he had essentially done the night of her headache. She couldn't quite seem to forgive him for that. So she was not pleased when, shortly after her arrival at her father's slightly dilapidated duplex, it became obvious that William had engineered this little family gathering.

Cassidy was leaning against the counter in her father's kitchen, staring out the window over the sink, when William's sensible sedan pulled into the drive behind her own little car. She knew at once that she'd been had. "That's it," she said, stepping back and slapping a hand against the countertop. "I'm out of here." She grabbed her purse from the seat of a nearby bar stool and slung it over her shoulder.

"Come on, Cass," Alvin Penno cajoled in his gravelly voice. He closed the oven door, having checked the hamburger patties spattering grease all over his broiler element, and pulled up his black leather jeans. "I know Will's a trial, but he is

our brother, and whatever's wrong between you obviously
eeds an airing.''

Cassidy shook her head in uncharacteristic stubbornness. ''I
ave nothing to say to William, and I don't care to hear what
e has to say to me.''

''He's pretty adamant in this, honey,'' Alvin warned her,
olding his bare arms over the leather vest he wore over a bare
hest. Cass noted a new tattoo beneath the motto on his upper
rm that read Bald is Beautiful, a small frog with a crown
erched upon his bald pate. ''Besides,'' Alvin pointed out,
'he's parked behind you.''

Trapped. Cassidy said a curse word she'd never before ut-
ered aloud in her whole life. Alvin was so shocked that his
and flew to the top of his bald head, his baldness having
one nothing to stop him from growing the hair below long
nough to wear it pulled back into a ponytail.

The back door squeaked as it opened and William walked
. ''Well,'' he said, targeting Cassidy at once, ''I've finally
n you to ground.'' He shook a finger at her. ''Now you're
oing to listen to what I have to say.''

''No, William, I'm not,'' Cassidy insisted flatly. ''What I
oose to do with my life is none of your business!''

And the battle was joined, William declaring that her be-
avior was threatening his job, despite her argument that Paul
ould never unfairly penalize an employee. They were shout-
g at each other as they hadn't done since childhood. Back
en William had almost always won their clashes due to the
ght years difference in their ages. But Cassidy was no longer
r brother's social and emotional inferior. She was at least
self-possessed as him and very likely more mature, which,
e had to admit, wasn't saying much. Nevertheless, she
ould not, could not, give him the upper hand in this. For the
st time since grade school, she actually gave as good as she
t from her brother. Something told her that more was at risk

here than her relationship with Paul, which was temporary a
best, and she doggedly refused to give ground.

Cassidy realized that William was not used to such a show
of strength from his little sister. He was, in fact, quite used to
bullying her with little effort. He couldn't know what to make
of the virago who met him toe-to-toe in their father's kitchen
bellowing her lungs out in self-defense, but she didn't care
She would not back down in this.

"My relationship with Paul, whatever it is, is none of your
business! You have no say in who I see, so just keep your
opinions to yourself!"

"For pity's sake, Cassidy, he's almost a married man!"

"He's not even an *engaged* man yet!"

"*Yet* being the operative word," William pointed out. "You
know he has to marry her!"

"So? He isn't married to her *now,* and even if he was, he
could still be my friend!"

"You're more than friends," William stated flatly. "I don't
know how it happened, but it almost looks like... It almost
looks like...he's in love with you!"

A flash of pleasure, wrapped in pain, struck Cassidy square
in the heart, so intense that she had to grab at her anger to
hold on to it. "So what if he were?" she managed. "I
wouldn't change anything! He'd still have to marry *her.*"

"My point exactly!"

"Then what are you worried about? Surely not a little thing
like my getting my heart broken!" She could tell from the
expression on his face that he hadn't given two seconds of
thought to the possibility that she might get hurt. Oh, no, all
his concern was for himself! "Well, relax, brother dear," she
said caustically. "Your plan to get Paul safely married to Be
tina is still intact!" William literally blanched, all the color
draining from his face in a snap. "Good heavens!" Cass ex
claimed, insight stunning her. "You're in this thing up to your
neck, aren't you? You're in this with Betina!"

Guilt wrote itself all over William. It was everywhere, in his eyes, the twist of his mouth, the flutter of his hands, the set of his shoulders, even the way one foot seemed to edge toward the door. His neck stretched, his head wobbling at the end. "I-I don't know what you mean. A-all I've ever done... all I've ever *wanted* was the best...for everyone!"

Cassidy could only stare, as if seeing him for the first time. He was utterly pathetic, her brother—frightened, unsure, even paranoid. He always expected the worst. Life was one long terror for him. All these years she had believed herself to be the weak one, while he had secretly feared...everything... everyone. Some of the anger left her, but not the resolve. "William," she said reasonably, firmly, "your job is not at risk, not from me. No matter how deeply you may be involved with Betina and her schemes."

He twisted miserably in place and blurted out, "I didn't mean to do it! Sh-she confided in me. She said she had to make him marry her. I didn't ask why! I didn't think it was my place!"

Cassidy sighed and shook her head. Poor William. "You told Betina that threatening the company was the only way to make Paul marry her." It was a statement, not a question, but he answered it, anyway, rather meekly.

"Yes."

"And who's idea was it to play hard-to-get?"

"Hers! And I advised against it *strongly*. But she wouldn't listen, just as she wouldn't listen when I advised her to play the part of his great-grandmother in our little drama."

Cassidy nodded. She didn't really want to know any more. All she really wanted— Tears scalded the backs of her eyes when she realized that all she really wanted was Paul. Squaring her shoulders, she lifted her chin. "He's going to marry her," she told William calmly, "because he doesn't have any choice. But that doesn't mean I'm going to stop seeing him."

William conceded miserably, bobbing his head. "Betina has

threatened to have me fired, you know, if for some reason he should not follow through.''

''That's not going to happen,'' she promised him. ''For one thing, he's going to marry her, and for another, I won't let it.''

Surprise sent his eyebrows skyward. ''You have that much influence?''

It was obvious that he didn't consider his question insulting. He just couldn't imagine his little sister having influence with anyone. She let it pass, saying only, ''Yes, I think I do.''

To her amusement, William struggled several moments to find something appropriate to say, finally coming up with ''Thank you.''

She chuckled. ''You're welcome. Now can we agree to close the subject, permanently?'' William shrugged. She took that for an affirmative answer, saying, ''Good. Now can we eat? I'm hungry.''

Alvin cleared his throat and, when they turned to him, pointed at the plate he'd heaped with burgers. ''Did someone say she was hungry?''

Cassidy had forgotten he was even there, or rather that she was here, in his house. She looked at her father with his tattoo and his leather and his bald-top ponytail, and it occurred to her that he hadn't interfered, hadn't demanded explanations or attention. He'd merely allowed her and William to air their differences. At least he treated them, her, like adults. Cassidy smiled and crossed the room to pull out a stool at the bar and park herself upon it. She looked a pointed invitation at William over her shoulder. Obediently William sat down, and Alvin served lunch, chatting about how he loved these greasy burgers and ''tater'' chips.

Alvin's theory was that since a fellow only lived once and he'd managed to make it to retirement, he was entitled to all the enjoyment he could handle from this point onward, and that included eating whatever he pleased. His inclinations were so counter to that of his ex-wife—who as she aged tended to become more and more intent on protecting herself in ever more bizarre ways—that they had led to, if not hastened, the divorce that ended their marriage of some thirty-two years.

Cassidy understood the necessity for the divorce, but William had always had a problem with it. He just didn't see why they couldn't have stayed married. So what if their approaches to this stage of their lives were diametrically opposed? As far as he was concerned they ought to just ignore that fact and carry on. He was embarrassed by them both, by Anna's determination to find the secret of longevity and Alvin's abandoned pursuit of enjoyment. Moreover, he didn't understand why they couldn't go their own ways and remain married. Cassidy, on the other hand, couldn't help wondering why they had stayed married as long as they had. It was easier for her to deal with them, but then she was beginning to see that it was easier for her to deal with life in general than it was her brother. That discovery somehow strengthened her, and she found herself enjoying, for the first time in a long time, the simple act of sharing a meal with members of her own family.

William stayed no longer than necessary, taking his leave as soon as he'd done justice to the food, oddly subdued and quiet. No doubt he was puzzled by the turn of events, by his sister's refusal to buckle under the pressure he had applied. Cassidy felt sorry for him, even as she realized that William would likely never know the kind of heartbreak to which she had willingly opened herself. After William had gone, Alvin boldly, bluntly leaped into Cassidy's business, saying, "Tell me about it." She didn't have to ask what he meant

"I'm in love with a man who has to marry someone else, and he just happens to be William's boss."

Alvin, bless him, didn't blink an eyelash. "Did he get her pregnant?"

"No!"

"Then why's he have to marry her?"

Cassidy sighed. "It's complicated. Let's just say that if he doesn't marry her, his business and his family will suffer greatly.

"Hmm, and is he in love with you?"

"Yes, I think he is—for now, anyway."

"Now's all there ever is, sweetheart. Now's all there ever is."

He was right, of course. While tomorrow would ever be a promise, and the past could never be relived, the present remained the only true reality. It made sense, then, especially if the future promised only loss, to grab all you could from the present.

"Why don't you tell me all about it?" Alvin urged gently.

Cassidy took a deep breath and began by explaining why Paul had to marry Betina Lincoln. Alvin merely grunted at that, either reserving or withholding judgment. When he had heard it all, or at least as much as she was willing to tell him, he had only one thing to say. "Well, kid, I'm proud of you. You could've crawled into a hole somewhere and pretended that what you two feel for each other never happened, but instead you've chosen to seize the moment and take all you can get from it. It may hurt like hell later, but you'll always have the memory of these days, and that's something."

It came to her suddenly that he was right. She could have Paul now or not at all, and not at all was no longer an option. She thanked her father for lunch, apologized for leaving him with the dishes and excused herself. As she slipped out the door, she heard him chuckle and mutter, "Damned if I didn't think that girl would live her whole life a virgin."

Embarrassment and humiliation burned her face red, but it only strengthened her resolve to take all she could from the present—and prove her father's previous assumptions about her false.

Chapter Seven

Paul smiled down at Cassidy, just as instructed in the script, and at the proper place in the narrative, slipped his arm about her, pulling her close. This time, however, Cassidy did more than simply stare up at him. She lifted her hand and stroked his cheek, her eyes full of promises that were anything but scripted. Paul's heart suddenly swelled. It was all he could do not to lower his head and kiss her, and then the light faded, and he groped for her hand in the dark, leading her carefully across the blackened stage as the lights came up elsewhere and the narration subtly shifted in tone. The new scene was that of the original Barclay Bakery, with patrons lining up to purchase the breads and pastries turned out by the Barclays and their small staff, but Paul didn't follow either the narration or the action as he led Cassidy backstage.

To his surprise, the moment they reached the relative privacy to be found behind the scene, Cassidy turned and slid her arms around his waist, squeezing him tightly. "Oh, I've missed you!" she whispered, adding, "You know, I've never slept so soundly as I did the night you stayed with me."

Paul felt his heart lurch inside his chest, a bittersweet joy filling him. He remembered the night he'd shared with her and the morning after. The feel of her beneath him had haunted him ever since, but he'd gone away with the impression that their brush with ultimate intimacy had left her shaken and even a little frightened. God knew that he couldn't blame her, and yet he'd tortured himself ever since with the certain knowledge that some other man would be the first to taste that particular joy with her, while he lived out a farce with a woman he couldn't bear to touch. He wondered now if life wasn't about to be more generous to him than he had any right to expect, but he put aside that thought in order to simply enjoy the moment. He leaned down and did what he had repeatedly wanted to do ever since he'd met this woman, he kissed her, quite thoroughly, and was rewarded with her full participation.

She was, in fact, a little aggressive, her arms looping about his neck and pulling tight, her mouth opening wide beneath his, her tongue stroking his before sliding into his mouth. She plastered her body to his, moaning. Paul was shaken, inflamed—and a little puzzled. She wasn't exactly throwing herself at him, but she wasn't behaving as he'd come to expect, either. He didn't know whether to be dismayed or delighted. Then she dropped a hand to his chest and rubbed it firmly up and down his torso in slow, yet oddly frantic strokes, and he was suddenly in the most exquisite pain. He throbbed with red-hot need, but it was more than physical and more than emotional. It was soul-deep yearning of a sort he'd never before felt—and never expected to feel again. He forgot to wonder what was going on and simply reveled in it.

Ah, Cassidy. Had he ever wanted a woman this much? Had he ever needed a woman's touch so desperately?

He lost track of his hands for a few seconds, then she gasped into his mouth, and he realized that he had cupped a breast and was kneading it and she had not pulled away. But if one of them didn't call a halt soon he was going to be opening zippers and heading for the floor. He wondered how long it would be before someone came looking for them and then conceded that it wouldn't be long enough. He wanted all her clothes off. Obediently his free hand began tugging the tail of her ribbed knit sweater free of her corduroys. It was then that she finally pulled back.

She stood with her hands on his forearms, gasping for breath and trembling. He curbed the impulse to reach for her again and just waited, hoping, dreaming, not daring to examine too closely what was happening here. Suddenly she lunged forward, grabbing his shirt front in her fists and blurting raggedly, "Come home with me tonight!"

He covered her hands with his. "Cass—"

"I want you to come home with me!"

"Aw, babe. What I wouldn't give—"

"Please! I need you, Paul. I know we can't be together very long, but I want as much of you as I can have as long as I can have it. Please."

He put his arms around her, holding her tight against him as he savored the moment. Gratitude filled him, humbling in its magnitude. "All right. If it's what you want."

"It is."

He closed his eyes and merely held her a moment longer. "Cass, I want you so much!"

She loosened her hold on his shirt, smoothing her hands across his chest. "Wait about half an hour," she whispered. "Then come."

He nodded. "Half an hour."

She pushed free of him and moved wraithlike toward the steps that led down onto the factory floor. Then suddenly she was back, her hands on his shoulders, her mouth pressing against his. "I love you!" she whispered breathlessly, rocking him to the soles of his feet.

"Cass—"

But she had fluttered away, her footfalls tapping lightly on the stairs.

He felt, suddenly, like laughing—or weeping—or both. Jerking his hands over his face, he took several deep breaths and tried to blank his mind, knowing it was the only way he'd make it through the remaining hour or more of rehearsal and that long thirty minutes before he could go to her, make love to her. Cassidy. His Cassidy. For now.

Zombielike he got through, not even remembering afterward what he'd done or said or seen. He was as aware of Cassidy's tension as his own but nothing and no one else. He couldn't even recall if she'd looked at him directly, if there had been unread messages in her soft green eyes. He remembered mostly the brightness of the lights and the slowly ticking seconds until he found himself standing in an empty parking lot, watching the small red taillights of the cars carrying away the others. One pair of them belonged to Cassidy's old German economy car, but he dared not seek them out even now. Instead he got into his own low-slung luxury model and drove to the nearest coffee shop, where he chugged down two cups and ate a piece of soggy pie that he didn't even want. Exactly twenty-eight minutes after he arrived, he got up and left again.

Oddly, now that the moment was nearly at hand, he felt a calmness settle over him that he hadn't expected. True, he was a man of experience, too much experience, for most of it he had reason to regret. He knew now why his grandfather had worried for him. He'd been spinning his wheels, running in place, getting nowhere fast, accomplishing nothing, following bodily urges blindly as if that were all this life had to offer. And then a funny, unaffected, bottom-shelf virgin, a lovely and unexpected treasure somehow overlooked by the rest of the world, had put him on the right path. He'd never beheld such a vista of beauty, never felt such accomplishment in simply making another person smile or hum or moan the way she had in his arms backstage. And she loved him! That was the most surprising and most humbling realization of all. She loved him, enough to give him what she had given no other man, even knowing that he could never walk that happy road to forever with her. If he was damned—and he was—then he was the luckiest damned man alive.

He pulled up at her curb in the brightest frame of mind he'd known since his grandfather had passed away, and found himself wishing that he could tell the old man how happy he was at this moment. But maybe he knew. Maybe they all knew, his parents right on down to Theo and Jane. Maybe they were sitting up there somewhere marveling at what they'd wrought. Or maybe they were shaking their heads over the mess he'd gotten himself into, over the waste his life would be after Cassidy. But he wouldn't think of that. Not now. Not when the next few hours promised such joy, enough, he hoped, to last him a lifetime.

He got out of the car, pocketed the keys and jauntily trotted up the pathway to the front door. He knocked and after several moments heard a sultry voice bid him enter. He turned the knob and stepped into fantasyland.

She'd draped the lamps with red scarves and strewn pillows over the floor. Candles flickered all around the perimeter of the room. Soft music played from…he wasn't sure where, and he didn't wonder beyond the moment she stepped up to his side and lifted her hands to the collar of his jacket.

"Let's get rid of this," she said silkily. He put his arms back and let her slip the jacket from his shoulders. She folded it and draped it carefully over the arm of the chair, and when she turned back to him he caught his breath, realizing suddenly what she wore—or rather, what she didn't wear.

Ribbed knit and corduroy had given way to a most unconventional costume. She was a French can-can dancer in figure-hugging black satin that closed down the front with a row of tiny silver hooks. Strapless, practically topless, it squeezed in at her tiny waist and pushed her amazingly generous breasts upward. A kind of bustle made of rows of sheer, ruffly fabric fanned out over her hips in the back, but her legs were left bare of all but the very sheerest black stockings seamed up the backs and held in place with white lacy garters at mid-thigh. She wore black shoes with sharp toes and stiletto heels and bows that had been tied at her wrists with strips of hot pink ribbon. Using the same ribbon, she'd caught her dark gold hair in a loose chignon at the crown of her head and left tendrils to float about her face and shoulders, and for the first time that he could remember, she was wearing conventional cosmetics, but only a few strokes of black mascara and sheer, glossy red lipstick.

She was breathtaking, exquisite. And his.

He reached for her. She put her hands in his and danced at the ends of his fingertips, smiling, beguiling. Then she came into his arms and began unbuttoning his shirt with slow, studied motions. Trembling, he bent his knees slightly and swept her into his arms. She slid her arms about his neck and bent her head to nuzzle his ear, whispering, "Maybe we should go on into the bedroom."

Flickering candles lit the way and surrounded the bed. She had exchanged the cotton sheets for creamy satin. The top sheet had been folded back to the foot of the bed. He sat her gently on the side and went down on his knees, tugging her shoes off and laying them aside, one by one. She leaned back on her hands and tossed her head, smiling as she lifted a leg. Reverently, he slipped his fingers beneath one lacy garter and slid it down her leg and over her foot, letting it fall before going back up to skim down the top of her stocking. When he reached her knee, he let his mouth follow the paths of his fingers until the stocking lay puddled on the floor and he nipped the arch of her foot with his teeth, his hands already searching for the second garter. The second stocking quickly followed the first, and then he rose, tugging her to her feet and bending his head to taste the bare skin of her shoulder while his hands followed the contours of her body to the row of hooks and eyes holding together that tantalizing black satin. When he found them, he lifted his head to watch what he was doing.

The hooks slid back, up, and out in small bunches, parting inches of fabric at a time until the stiff, boned bodice and fluttery bustle fell away, leaving her clad only in a tiny pair of black panties that made his heart skip beats and speed up. He ran trembling hands over naked skin, forgetting to breathe. He filled his hands with her breasts and closed his eyes, feeling the weight and the warmth of them transmitted to every cell in his body.

"Sweet heaven!" he gasped, looking down at her again. "You're not just beautiful, you're the most—"

But she was even more than that, more than he could put into words. She was incredible. She was perfection. She was everything woman and everything lover and everything innocence—and she deserved far more than he could give her. She deserved a man who wouldn't be just first but forever. And it wasn't him. Thanks to his own stupidity and Betina's obsessive needs, he could not be the man Cassidy Penno deserved, and that she loved him despite that fact made the situation even worse. He could love her as no other man could, but he couldn't give her what she deserved most, and because he couldn't give her what she deserved, he couldn't take what he did not deserve.

The tears caught him by surprise, spilling over his cheeks before he even knew they were there. He lifted a hand to his face and felt the roughness of his beard. He hadn't even shaved for her. While she had been here arranging the perfect love nest, he'd been selfishly counting the seconds until he could show up and claim what she so lovingly offered, even knowing that he had nothing to offer in return. But he knew now that he loved her more than he'd realized. He loved her even more, if such a thing was possible, than he wanted her. The knowledge was shattering and somehow empowering because it gave him the strength to do what he'd never thought he could. It gave him the strength to stop.

Sighing, he closed his eyes and said, "I can't."

Cassidy leaned into him, confused, her slender arms wrapping around him. "Paul? Paul, what's wrong? Did I do something—"

"No." He shook his head. "No, no." He put his arms around her, achingly aware of all that smooth, bare skin, a distraction, to put it mildly. He yanked his shirt free and whipped it off, settling it gently over her shoulders. Tenderly, he worked her arms into the sleeves and buttoned it up. All the while, she tried to talk to him.

"Please, tell me what's wrong. Whatever it is, we can fix it. I know we can. Please, Paul, listen to me. I thought about this a long time. I know what I'm doing, and I think you want this, too. Don't you? Or am I wrong?"

"You're not wrong," he told her finally. "I am."

She pushed at the cuffs hanging over her hands and said, "What?"

He looked at her. She was understandably confused, adorably cute, more dear than anything or anyone he'd ever seen, and he knew that if he didn't get her out of this candlelit bedroom right this moment he would lose what little good sense he possessed. He turned her toward the door and ushered her quickly down the hall and back into the living room, where he sank down on the sofa and put his head in his hands, sighing.

"I don't understand," she said, coming to sit beside him.

He smiled at that. "I know."

"Why did you stop?"

He dropped his hands and tilted his head in order to look her in the face. "Because I love you."

Her whole face softened, and her eyes misted, her lower lip trembling. "Oh, Paul!"

He put his arm around her, and together they leaned back on the sofa, her head on his shoulder. "I'm sorry, babe," he told her softly. "I didn't know what I was getting us into. I never dreamed... Well, let's just say I've discovered that love doesn't leave room for selfishness."

"What selfishness? I asked you to come. I want you to—"

He derailed that, knowing where it was going. "And I want to, but I can't. It's not enough just to be the first, Cass. I thought it would be, but it's not. Honey, you're the kind of woman who needs and deserves everything a man has to give—his name, his children, his forever after." He took a deep breath, ignored the straining and thickening of his voice and made himself go on. "That's not me. I wish it was, but it's not. Somewhere out there is a man who'll be your one and only, and I won't rob you of that just to be your first, not even if it kills me."

She sat up then and twisted around to face him, one leg curled beneath her. "Don't cry," she whispered, and he laughed because he hadn't known that he was and because what else was there to do?

"I won't if you won't," he said, and she wiped her face with the cuffs of his shirt.

"Why'd it have to be like this?" she asked.

He steeled himself and said, "Because I cheated us, and I didn't even know I was doing it. I screwed it up before it even had a chance to happen."

"I don't care," she told him in a trembling voice.

"I know, but I do. I care because I love you. More than I ever thought possible. So much that I'm going now before this attack of decency passes."

"Don't talk like that," she said as he stood and moved to the chair to take up his jacket. "You're not a bad person."

He slung the jacket on over his bare back and turned up the

collar. "No, but I haven't been a good one, either, not like you."

"Oh, Paul."

"I have to go."

"Don't you want your shirt?" she asked, going up on her knees and reaching for the buttons. She was tempting him, and he loved her for it. She looked like an angel who had lost her wings. He shook his head.

"Naw, you keep it. That way I can torture myself by thinking of you in it."

"Paul, please, please stay."

But they both knew he couldn't. He opened the door and looked down at her one last time. "Goodbye, Cass. And thank you."

He made sure to lock the door before he pulled it shut behind him, just in case she didn't remember to get up and set the dead bolt. "Ah, God," he said, hearing her sobs. Before he could change his mind, he hurried down the walk to his car, digging for the key in his pants pocket. By the time he got the engine started and was safely away, his own tears were coming fast again, but he knew that for once he'd done the right thing for someone else at his own expense, and that someone was Cassie. No one mattered more.

He didn't sleep. At all. Not a blink. After the first ten minutes, he didn't even try. Instead he got up, put on a pair of warm-up bottoms and sat in his den drinking coffee, lots and lots of coffee. Around daybreak he showered and tried to eat, but the granola he tried to force down his throat turned his stomach. He dressed and went into the office early. It was a bad, bad day for Betina to try pushing his buttons.

She did not, of course, take no for an answer. She ignored his secretary's warning and swept straight into his office. Groomed to within an inch of her life, her blond hair twisted into a smooth, dignified chignon, she posed herself on the corner of his desk, crossed her willowy legs and gave him what passed for a smile, careful, as always, that it did not wrinkle the corners of her eyes. They were expertly made up eyes, but then her makeup consultant was a true artist.

He leaned back in his black leather executive chair and looked her over head to toe, noting the expensive, pale pink suit with its slim, above-the-knee skirt and sexy, single-button jacket worn without a blouse. Her stylish, square-toed shoes were the exact same shade as the suit. No doubt she'd had them dyed. The oversize pearls at her throat and earlobes picked up the shade and reflected it lovingly, lending a creamy tone to her skin. Pity she was a selfish, unlovable witch. Compared to Cassidy, Betina was a cold, bloodless viper, a demon in pink, as opposed to Cassidy's angel in black satin. Just the thought of black satin would torture him forever more. And for it he could thank the smug seductress trying to flash him a look up her skirt without being too obvious about it. She made him ill—and angry, angrier than he had ever been before.

"Get out of my sight," he said, pivoting away from her. He felt her shock. Seldom was he so blatant about his feelings, not since dear old Granddad had dropped the noose around his neck and put the end of the rope into her hand. He almost wished she'd yank and be done with it, but he reminded himself that he had responsibilities to the family and the business. Funny, they didn't seem to mean anymore what they once had. Nothing did.

Betina got off the corner of his desk and walked around his chair to place herself right in his line of sight. He averted his eyes. "I can always call Security and have you thrown out," he said.

He expected her to spit and scream, but instead she adopted a studied nonchalance. "I spoke to William."

He closed his eyes, imagining what William might have told her, and made up his mind that if she said one negative word about Cassidy, he'd throw her out of the office himself—and enjoy it. But Betina was nothing if not intelligent. She apparently recognized a man who was skating on the thin edge of composure when she saw him. He knew that the dark circles beneath his eyes and the lines of strain around his mouth signaled an inner struggle of immense proportion. Of course, she couldn't know what had happened between him and Cassidy—or what hadn't—but she had to realize that she just might have pushed too far for once. She at least wanted to appear gracious in capitulation.

"I've been thinking about it," she said, "and I-I've decided Will is right. I was foolish to turn down a part written especially with me in mind, and I want you to know…I'll play the part."

Paul shook his head, grimly amused that she could be moved by any inducement to put her image at such risk. William must have convinced her that she was in real danger of losing the game, after all. Ah, God, if only he could walk away from it. If it was just the job, just the business, at stake, he'd do it without a second thought or a glance back, but the family deserved consideration. They depended on him. They were totally dependent on Barclay Bakeries for income, and Barclay supported them well. Moreover, he had sworn, literally, to look after their interests. For the first time, it felt as if Hool was right, as if Paul's family took gross advantage of him. He reminded himself that it hadn't felt that way before, but then everything had changed since Cassidy had come into his life. He told himself wearily that the only way to change it back again was to cut out Cass entirely—and knew he couldn't do it. But Betina could and wouldn't think twice about it. Perhaps it was best that way for all concerned.

"Suppose you toddle along and talk to William about it," he said caustically. "He seems to care. I don't. Goodbye."

Still, she stayed. "You're in a strange mood. Anything can do?"

He was on his feet and backing her toward the door before he even knew that he intended to move. "Yes!" he snarled. "Stay the hell out of my way. I don't want to see you. I don't want to talk to you. I don't want to *think* about you!"

"What about the practices?" she asked, her voice unnaturally high.

"*William* will fill you in. Apparently he's good at that!"

She recovered her aplomb the moment before they reached the door and walked out with her nose high and her stride regal. He closed the door and laid his head against the cool burled wood. *Cassidy, oh, Cassie.* Now there were no more excuses, not even to hold her one more time.

He was not so craven as to let William deliver the news. That particular punishment he reserved for himself, but he didn't have the strength to do it in person. Instead, he called Cass on the telephone at the shop. The false brightness of her tone cut him to the quick, and in as few words as possible he explained that Betina would be playing the part of Jane in their little Barclay Bakeries history drama. The silence at the other end of the line was rife with disappointment, but eventually she seemed to find her voice and calmly told him that it was for the best. Conversely he felt a stab of disappointment at her easy acquiescence. Some part of him wished she'd fight a little harder, maybe even overcome his own best intentions. That was absurd, of course. This was best, best for Cassidy, so he simply whispered, "I'm sorry," and hung up.

After a long day during which he accomplished nothing, he decided to skip practice and work late. Let William stand in for him. William seemed to be managing a goodly portion of his life for him, anyway. He'd just call and tell old William to manage on. But he didn't. He sat and stared at the phone until he was quite certain that William was no longer in the building, then he got up and drove straight to the old factory. Cassie's car was parked in its customary spot directly un-

derneath the light pole. Paul told himself that he dreaded seeing her, but he knew himself for a liar the moment he set foot
on the graveled parking lot. He could not wait to see her.
He was starving for a mere glimpse of her. The tremulous
smile she gave him as he came through the door afforded him
the first moment of peace that he had felt since leaving her
the night before. She had survived. She was hurting, true, but
all that was Cassidy was alive and well. He might never be
the same, but she would be. After all, angels were eternal.

He let his eyes feast as he walked over to join the group.
Her hair was pinned up almost exactly as it had been the night
before, but this time she wore a dark green turtleneck sweater
belted over a bias-cut plaid wool skirt that reached almost to
her booted ankles. Around her neck she wore a long necklace
of large, colored wood beads. She looked fragile and dainty,
despite her height, and he felt acutely the loss of the freedom
to put his arms around her.

Betina, on the other hand, looked like a sleek, pitiless pred-
ator in a dark red pantsuit of body-hugging knit with a flared
jacket that zipped up the front. She'd let down her hair and
combed it into a smooth flip, very chic, very cutting edge.
Paul entertained himself with the notion that she might slip
and cut her own throat, but before he could enjoy the scenario
too much, Cassidy called everyone to order, announced in a
strained voice that William would be handling rehearsals from
now on, and quickly departed to "other duties." It was Tony
who stepped forward, once she was out of earshot, and demanded an explanation.

"You don't know anything about theater," he said to William. "Why should we listen to you?"

William clearly disliked having his ability or his authority
questioned. He scoffed at Tony's concern. "We're not exactly
interpreting Shakespeare here, Abatto, and I did help write the
script. Besides, if Cassidy thinks I'm capable of guiding the
production, I don't see what you have to say about it."

"I'm not so sure Cassidy is cool with this," Tony insisted, glaring at William. "She's been upset all day, and then this afternoon I caught her crying. Then she tells me that she's not going to play the part of Jane, after all."

"I'm afraid that's my fault," Betina said smoothly, stepping forward.

William leapt to her side, announcing her as if she were royalty. "Ms. Betina Lincoln will now play the part of Jane. It was, after all, written especially for her."

Betina smiled at that and said without a trace of self-effacement, "At first I thought the role was beyond me, but eventually I realized that it was truly in all our best interests for me to take my rightful place."

Paul could only shake his head at that bit of sleight of hand. Tony didn't quite buy it, either. "That doesn't explain this morose mood of Cassidy's. I can't believe it's as simple as Miss Lincoln deciding to stand in as Jane."

"I'm not a stand-in," Betina said crisply. "The part was written for me."

William shot a look at Paul, who felt as though his face was set in stone. William seemed to take that for carte blanche and came to a poor decision, at Cassidy's expense. "My sister is a very gifted individual, but her imagination sometimes runs away with her and the resultant crash with reality is always painful. She'll be all right in a day or two. You'll see."

If he'd left it at that, Paul might have made it through the evening, but even as he sent the others to their places, William stepped up to Paul and sealed his own fate. "You know, I must apologize to you. I sensed some time ago that Cass had developed a crush on you—"

"A crush?" Paul echoed disbelievingly.

"I know, I know," William went on, completely missing Paul's meaning. "I should have spoken to you about it right away, but somehow I let myself be convinced that it was mutual, but then after that little scene backstage yesterday, I knew I had to do something—"

"You heard us? You *listened?*"

"It was painfully obvious what she intended, and perhaps I shouldn't have gone to Betina with the information, but of course, I couldn't know at the time that you were planning to turn her down. When she told me this morning...well, all I can say is that perhaps in future she'll think twice before she throws herself at a man so obviously beyond her."

Rage such as he had never known seized Paul. To think that William had stood there in the darkness and listened to them plan to make love and then to know that Paul had walked out on her... That he had taken the news to Betina was incidental, though it explained her sudden change of mind concerning the role of Jane, but the thought that William—smarmy, unctuous, icy William—had witnessed both Cassidy's bold generosity and her despair was enough to make Paul react with a violent urge he never knew he had.

Paul reached up with one hand and clamped it around William's throat. Ignoring the harsh cry that gurgled out of William's mouth, Paul lifted him off the ground. "You stupid, insensitive son of a bitch. I ought to rip your throat out. Don't you dare talk about your sister as if she was some pathetic spinster desperately misreading the interest of every man she meets! If I ever hear you speak of her in such a manner again I'll break you into so many pieces they'll never find them all! Do you understand me?"

William managed a nod, his eyes bulging for lack of air. Only after he'd dropped him, choking and coughing, to the floor did Paul realize that he was surrounded by babbling voices and shocked faces. He looked around at the wary group watching him with wide eyes and found that he possessed neither the energy nor the emotion to give a flip what they thought of him or his actions. He sent one cold look at Betina, announced flatly that rehearsal was canceled, calmly stepped over William and headed for the door.

To hell with them all. Let them think whatever they liked, Betina included. No, Betina *especially*. He was through rolling over and playing dead for her. That was odd, for now that he felt dead inside, he found he couldn't pretend even minimally to care what she thought, said or did. He would do what he had to, including marry her if she insisted, and he had no doubt that she would, but never would he let her or anyone else believe for a moment that he could feel for her even a fraction of what he felt for Cassidy Penno. If a forced marriage was what she wanted, a forced marriage was what she'd get and not a damned iota more. She could have her wedding, and then they'd both live in hell. He had already moved in, and for once he didn't care if she moved in with him.

Chapter Eight

Paul's mood did not lighten. After the fiasco at practice it was decided—he didn't ask by whom—that the schedule would be revised to just one night a week. After all, as Betina put it, there were precious few lines to learn and William had talked her through the part already. She made it sound as if it were a walk in the park beginning to end, as if research hadn't been done, a script written, scenes designed, stages built, props found, parts assigned, blocking established, costumes created, lighting and sound provided and a good deal of direction already received. Cassidy had done all the hard, creative work; now Betina walked in, snagged the spotlight and derided all that had gone before. If he'd had more energy and if speaking Cassidy's name to Betina hadn't felt like desecration, he'd have set the witch straight on a few things, but lately it was all he could do just to get through the days. The nights... The nights were an agony he could only endure.

The night of his uncle John's sixty-third birthday was no exception. Paul would have forgotten it completely if Carl, John's brother and Betina's stepfather, had not reminded Paul that he'd offered his home for the family celebration. Reluctantly, Paul went through the motions of organizing a dinner party, which consisted of informing his housekeeper and cook that they would be eight for dinner and calling down to the specialty bakery to have a cake decorated in honor of the occasion. He picked up the cake on his way home from work, then stopped by the liquor store and bought four bottles of champagne. Luckily the housekeeper had ordered a flower arrangement for the dinner table. Paul started upstairs intending to shower and change, but he passed the liquor cabinet on his way and decided it wouldn't hurt to begin bracing himself for an evening spent in company with Betina and the family. He was fairly well "braced" by the time his cousin Joyce Spencer Thomas and her husband, Cal, arrived, beaming like a pair of thousand-watt bulbs.

Joyce couldn't keep her exultation to herself. She refused the drink that Paul offered her, sent a gleefully conspiratorial look at her husband and blurted that she was, at last, pregnant. Uncle Carl and Aunt Jewel Barclay arrived right on the heels of the announcement, bringing with them Betina's regrets, and Paul found himself in the mood for a real celebration. He broke out the champagne immediately, brushing aside suggestions that perhaps they ought to wait for the honoree and Joyce's mother Mary to arrive. If anyone noticed Paul had already imbibed twice as much alcohol as was characteristic, no one said so. By the time dinner was actually served, he was feeling rather mellow. Unfortunately *mellow* became *maudlin* as talk centered on Joyce and Cal's impending new arrival.

"Just think," Mary Spencer gushed, still basking in the joy of the announcement, "I'm actually going to be a grandmother!"

Jewel sent a hopeful glance in Paul's direction and said meaningfully, "Perhaps next year we'll *both* be grandparents!"

Paul snorted into his glass. "As if Betina would sacrifice her figure for a child! No, no, face it, Aunt Jewel. You'll never be a grandmother. I'll never be a father. We are sacrifices at the shrine of Betina's obsession, you and I, sacrifices. Yes, that about sums it up, sacrifices."

He didn't notice the appalled silence that fell over the assembly as he drained his glass and reached for the champagne bottle again. He had not touched his dinner. The scampi and medallions of beef looked appetizing enough, but he simply hadn't managed to get to it yet. Perhaps if he could slake his thirst...

John took it upon himself to change the subject. "How is the business? Things going well? I only ask because you seem, well, troubled."

Paul waved a hand dismissively. "We'll know better after the first of the year. I'd be hopeful except for all the interference I'm getting. It's damned irritating to have someone work against your every decision." Everyone knew who that someone was. He didn't have to identify her. Looks were traded.

Jewel focused on her plate. Carl cleared his throat and said heartily, "Well, I'm sure things will come right once you and Betina are married. She'll forget about dabbling in the business and focus on you." He smiled almost apologetically at his wife and received a hand squeeze for it. That seemed to give him the incentive to go on. "Love does that to a woman," he said.

Paul set his glass down with a thunk. "Love! Love? Are you insane?" The very idea of him and Betina being in love was absurd to the point of hilarity. So he laughed. And laughed. Until he saw the look on Aunt Jewel's face. Poor Aunt Jewel, with a daughter like Betina, she was bound to live a life full of disappointment. God knew she'd tried to be a good mother, but serpents made lousy daughters—and wives—which was nothing to laugh about. He sighed and reached for his glass again, tossing back the contents in a single gulp. His head buzzed for several moments, the sound seeming to come from behind his eyes. He rubbed them with the heels of his palms, wanting nothing so much as a moment's peace. When he looked up again, the sound receding, it was to find his aunt and uncle both staring at him in near horror.

Jewel placed her hands on either side of her plate, intently forming her words. "Paul, are you saying… That is, you're sincere when you say…when you *imply* that you and…that you aren't in love?"

He closed his eyes and pressed his fingertips to his temples, which were aching vaguely. He really didn't have the time or the energy for this. "Aunt Jewel," he said, striving for the right note, "you can't honestly believe that Betina and I are a love match."

"But you were…uh, last year you were…"

"Having an affair?" he finished for her impatiently. "Yes, well, she managed that beautifully. In fact, she parlayed it into marriage by blackmail." His temples were throbbing now, and gall burned the back of his throat. He began to wonder if he wasn't going to embarrass himself in front of his dinner guests. Better wrap this up. He got to his feet, swaying slightly, and proclaimed, "Don't worry, I'll marry her." He looked around the table, vaguely aware that the expressions that greeted him were troubled. He sighed and moved away from the table, muttering. "For your sakes, I'll marry her, and for your sakes I'll keep her greedy, interfering little paws out of the business. A sacrifice," he said to himself. "I'm your damned sacrifice." He left them sitting there and climbed the stairs, intent upon nothing more than making it to his bedroom before he passed out—or worse.

He looked at the glass of fizzing, hissing bromide on his desk and remembered again why he usually confined his alcohol consumption to a single drink per occasion. Had his head been smaller or his gut made of something other than cold rubber, he'd have worried about the family's reaction, but even on his best days lately he couldn't quite seem to care as much as he should about the things he should. The intercom on his speaker phone buzzed and Gladys's frantic voice split his skull.

"Miss Lincoln is here, and she won't—" the door crashed open; Betina strode through it and slammed it again "—listen. I tried to tell her you couldn't be disturbed, but—"

Ignoring Betina, Paul depressed the send button on the intercom, cutting off Gladys and saying cryptically, "My fault. I should've bought you a gun."

Gladys's voice buzzed right back at him. "Sir?"

"It was a joke, Gladys. Unfortunately I'm not in a joking mood. Never mind."

He lifted the glass hissing at him from his blotter and leaned back in his chair, allowing his gaze to drift to Betina. He lifted both brows. Or was it Betina hissing at him? He wondered what he'd done to provoke such venom, never doubting that she would soon inform him. He saluted her with the glass, held his breath and glugged back the contents. "Ack!" Horrid stuff.

She threw herself at the desk, both hands smacking its surface. "How dare you?"

He waved a hand negligently and plunked down the empty glass. "Just lucky I guess."

She swung out and slapped the glass to the floor. It bounced harmlessly off the thick carpet and landed on its side, rolling in a lazy circle. For some reason he enjoyed that. He turned his gaze casually back to Betina, completely unmoved by her seething anger. She spun away, arms folding dramatically.

"You humiliated me in front of the whole family last night!"

"Really? I don't recall that you were even in the room."

She rounded on him. "How dare you tell my parents that you don't love me!"

He almost laughed. Apparently she wasn't upset that he didn't love her, merely embarrassed that the family should know. He shook his head. "I'm afraid you're in for a terrible disappointment if you expect me to play the lovesick hubby. I'm through with games of pretend. Get used to it."

"And I'm through being reasonable!"

"You were being reasonable? When? I missed it. Must've blinked."

In a grand gesture, she swept papers and picture frames from his desk, artfully furious. Paul leaned back in his chair and linked his hands behind his head, feeling a little better now that the bromide was taking effect.

"We could've done this civilly!" she hissed. "But you're determined to provoke me, first with your buy-out offers, then with little Miss Penno, and now this!"

He rocked forward, forearms hitting the desktop. All the humor had fled at the mention of Cassidy's name. "You leave her out of this."

Betina grinned ferally. "That's exactly what I intend to do, darling, and I intend to get it in writing!"

"What the hell are you talking about?"

"I'm talking about a detailed, iron-clad prenuptial agreement."

He smirked. Two could play at this game. "Excellent idea."

"Just remember, you brought this on yourself!" she exclaimed, sweeping toward the door. "Clause number one will state that, as far as you're concerned, from the day, the *hour*, we marry, Cassidy Penno ceases to exist!" With that she flung open the door and swept through it, leaving it open in her wake.

Paul stared at the empty door, uncertain whether to laugh or cry. As if there had ever been any question of his subjecting Cassidy to the sewer that would be his life after he married

Betina. Cassidy was made for better things, and God willing, she would get them—so long as he stayed away from her, and he would just as soon as the ball was over. They were never alone anymore; he saw to that. Soon he would be nothing but a memory to Cassidy, and one day probably not even that. She would find another man, someone who hadn't screwed up his life to the point that it was completely out of his control, someone who could give her everything she deserved, someone who could love her and stand by her always. But it could not be him. Betina needed no prenuptial agreement to see to that. He'd already taken care of it. Betina was right about one thing, though: he'd brought it all on himself.

Paul sat on the edge of the stage, following Cassidy with his eyes as she directed Hoot in the placement of the tables. Thanks to that brilliant mind of hers, Hoot had agreed not only to provide them with tables, chairs, dishes and flatware but to cater the meal, as well, and he was being paid handsomely for it. Paul even suspected that his friend had had a hand in picking out the band, too, for they were a large, rowdy orchestra who could swing effortlessly from waltzes to obscure turn-of-the-century tunes to jazz and everything in between with a distinctly bluesy big band sound. They were costing him a fortune, but they were worth it. This party was going to be a grand success, thanks almost entirely to Cassidy. His heart contracted at just the sight of her. God, what he wouldn't give to make Betina Lincoln a figment of his imagination.

The nonfigment entered the building just then with her usual door-slamming style. Her mid-calf, white fur, swing coat swirled around her legs as she stalked on absurdly high heels toward him. She carried a sheaf of papers in one hand, a look of sheer rage on her carefully made-up face. He knew exactly what this was about. So she had finally been to see the lawyer. Good. He was almost eager for the fight.

"How dare you!" she hissed, throwing the papers at his

face. Paul blocked them with a casually lifted hand and let them fall where they would.

"Gee, Betina, you seem a little out of sorts. Something I've done? I hope."

The entire room had stopped to stare, Hoot quite blatantly. It was Cassidy who cleared her throat and muttered something about giving Mr. Spencer and Miss Lincoln some privacy. Paul shook his head. "Oh, no. People are working here. Besides, I wouldn't dream of depriving Miss Lincoln of her public scene."

"You son of a—"

"Such a dignified response," Paul chided, grinning like the cat who ate the canary. Betina immediately curbed her temper, aware that she was not making any points or influencing anyone, which had clearly been her intent. With some effort, she turned anger to victimization.

"How could you make such a blatant grab for the company shares that Grandfather left me?"

"He was *my* grandfather," Paul pointed out wryly, "and how dare you blackmail me with the shares he left you, hmm?"

Betina had the grace to look uncomfortable. "I will not agree to give you my shares when we marry."

"No? Well, I refuse to let you hang on to them and hold them over my head every time we disagree. Evidence to the contrary, I'm not a complete idiot."

Her hands tightened into fists. "All right," she said, knowing some concession was in order. "You get to vote them—as long as we're married. In the event of a divorce, they revert back to me."

He'd expected that, but it galled him nonetheless. She couldn't resist turning the screw. She wanted the power to punish him if everything didn't go her way. He ground his teeth together, fighting to maintain his composure. "Let's try this another way. Let's say that when we marry, your shares will be divided between the family members, myself excluded, and that is where they will remain, whatever the state of our marriage. Can we agree to that, at least?''

Betina narrowed her eyes, and he had the chilling suspicion that he'd walked straight into a trap. ''Agreed,'' she said, ''provided you guarantee me an income for life.''

Paul slid off the edge of the stage. Landing lithely on the floor, he stepped close and spoke hotly. ''For pity's sake, if all it's about is money, then why not just let me buy your shares and forget this ridiculous marriage notion? I'll even guarantee you income for life as part of the deal!''

Betina smiled sweetly. ''And let you off the hook?'' Her gaze slid to Cassidy, who, apparently urged by Hoot, had moved closer. ''Not on your life, lover boy.''

Paul wanted to choke her. He went so far as to lay hands on her, grasping her by the shoulders. ''Damn you!'' he swore, pitching his voice low. ''She has nothing to do with this!''

Betina twisted out of his grasp, sneering, ''You're so right. You'll marry me, damn you, because I say you will!''

''Why? What could you possibly want with a husband who doesn't love you?''

She drew herself up. ''I have my pride, you know. I couldn't hold up my head in public, if you didn't marry me!''

''That's what this is all about? You've told your friends that we will marry and so we must?''

''Of course I have, you idiot!'' she hissed. ''Paul Barclay Spencer, heir apparent to the Barclay empire, most eligible bachelor in Dallas! Who else would make a more suitable wife to you than me? Not that insipid little nobody who spends her time playing dress-up—''

He grabbed the lapels of her coat and yanked her forward. ''One more word about her and I toss you out on your expensive fanny. And while we're on the subject, let me assure you that marriage to me will be anything but flattering to your image. I couldn't care less about your pride. Why should I, when you've stripped me of mine? Not that you have any, holding an entire family's welfare hostage in order to force a man who despises you to the altar! I promise you you'll regret this lunacy."

"Oh, really? And just how do you think to manage that?"

"I'm not completely powerless, Betina, whatever you may think. I may have to marry you, but I won't dance to your tune ever again. Let the world make of that what they will."

For the first time Betina looked worried. "What do you mean?"

Paul dropped his hands and backed away. Smiling, he beckoned toward Cassidy. "For starters," he said to Betina, and then he pitched his voice loud to address the room at large. "Can I have your attention, everyone? We find ourselves faced with yet another change." He smiled and lifted his arms as if to say that it couldn't be helped. "Miss Lincoln finds that she is unable to play the part of Jane, after all." Beside him, Betina gasped, but a glance in her direction showed him that, though pained, her smile was in place. She would not protest. She couldn't afford to. He looked to Cassidy and knew with no contrition at all that he'd just been waiting for an excuse to do this, any excuse to be close to her again. "Cass," he said evenly, "I guess you'll just have to fill in."

For a moment he held his breath, wondering if she would exercise her good sense and refuse, but she merely nodded and turned away, speaking softly to Hoot. Paul clapped his hands together. "Excellent. Well, now that that's settled, let's get to work." He pointed at his friend, noting that he still stood protectively at Cassidy's side. "Hoot, you'll enjoy this. Pull up a chair." He turned a raised eyebrow at Betina. Would she stay and watch, or would she go? She spun in a swirl of white fur and made for the door, calling over her shoulder, "I'll see you later...darling."

"Not if I see you first," he muttered through his teeth. When he looked down again, it was to find Cassidy at his side, a worried expression weighting her lovely eyes. He recognized the look. She was worried for him. Impulsively he found her hand and squeezed it, saying softly, "It's all right, love, as all right as it can be."

She studied him a moment longer, and then she nodded and turned away. "Everyone to your places. Let's move it! This is our last chance to iron out the wrinkles. Next rehearsal is dress rehearsal."

His lady had risen to the occasion again, God love her. It was certain that he already did. Oh, yes, he did, and he no longer cared who knew it. Betina's pride be damned.

Cassidy didn't know what to think. Was Paul having second thoughts? Was this self-imposed estrangement as difficult for him as for her? She prayed it was so and feared that it was at the same time. Even if Paul relented and spent time with her again, private time, what good would it do? They could not be together without wanting completion, without tumbling into each other's arms and bed. Would Paul abandon his lofty principles and love her during the little time they had left? How would she bear it, then, when it was over? She had walked through the days and nights without him like a zombie. It was as if her nerve endings had been seared and she could feel nothing but the emptiness, nothing but the loss.

And yet, here she was, standing next to him as if it was where she belonged, oddly at ease as they pantomimed the motions required by the narrative. She felt strangely at peace as if all had come right with her world, and knew it for the calm before the storm. She would lose him irrevocably, and then she would die, if not in body, then in spirit. She neither fought nor railed against the probability. She welcomed it in a bizarre fashion, praying that if she could not feel joy she would simply not feel at all. It seemed the only way to survive what was coming.

The first scene drew to a close. She stood next to Paul

feeling his arm come around her, laying her head against his shoulder in a gesture of trust and support. He looked down into her eyes, and she saw there all the love she could ever hope to possess and knew she was without hope to possess it. The narrator increased the volume of his voice to a crescendo. In moments the stage would grow dark and the scene would end.

Something drew her gaze to Paul's mouth. She recognized in the way he flattened and set it what was on his mind and mechanically turned up her face. His mouth settled on hers with all the drama and poignancy of the scripted moment. Her senses came alive. Like Sleeping Beauty throwing off the paralysis of sleep, she was plunged into a world of reality so sharp and focused that the perception of it was very nearly painful—and dearly welcome. Just before the lights went down to dark, a collective gasp penetrated the aura of sensation that suddenly bound her. People began to applaud. Paul broke the kiss but threw his arms around her, holding her close.

"Cassidy," he whispered. "Aw, sweetheart, forgive me."

She sobbed a little laugh. "For what?"

He never answered her. The lights suddenly snapped on, all of them. Cassidy lifted a hand to shield her eyes and peered past the tables to the flimsily constructed control booth, glimpsing William, his harried expression almost comical. Poor William. How many times must he deal with the same crisis? His boss was in love with his little sister and vice versa, a fact none of them seemed capable of outrunning. It was Tony's voice that snagged the lion's share of her attention, however.

"What the devil was that? That isn't in the script!"

"It is now," Paul answered vaguely. Cassidy turned her head to find him looking at her with those worshipful eyes, and she merely smiled, sadly, resignedly.

So human, her Paul. Despite his best intentions, he couldn't let go any more than she could, but one of them had to. Another scene with Betina like the one just played out and Paul would lose everything most dear to him...because of her. How could she let that happen? She couldn't, of course, not to the man she loved. She just couldn't.

He made up his mind, and the relief was staggering, now that it was a perfect solution. Far from it. He would be going back on his word and giving up his life's work, but to do otherwise would mean sacrificing Cassidy and her love, and that he simply could not do. So he was resigned. But still a chance remained, and honor demanded that he wait for it. Never again would he deny what he felt for Cassidy or attempt to hide it. Tonight, in fact, he would all but proclaim it. Let Betina try to cover that with her friends, if she could. His hope was that she could not. Perhaps if his preference for Cassidy became common knowledge, Betina's pride would be so stung that she would forget her scheme to marry Barclay Bakeries and settle for a generous buy-out instead. It was worth a shot, and his plan had the added bonus of allowing him to keep Cassidy close by his side all night.

It had been two days since he'd seen her. During that time, every moment had been given to the private appointments scheduled with the representatives of national grocery chains and their distributors. Those meetings, though brief, had gone quite well. He had made certain to include Cal Thomas, Cousin Joyce's husband, in as many of those meetings as possible. Cal, after all, might well find himself unexpectedly manning the helm of Barclay Bakeries one day soon.

Arriving early, Paul rigged himself in his costume for the evening and anxiously awaited Cassidy. Hoot was already there with his staff, banging pots and pans in the makeshift kitchen set up for him. The security team and parking valets were next on the scene, and right on their heels the band began to filter in. Paul wandered over and spent a nervous quarter hour plinking on the piano before the keyboardist arrived.

Betina came in wearing her white fur. Beneath it she was garbed in pale pink beaded with gold, her bare arms adorned with long matching gloves and heavy bracelets, her swirling skirts worn without petticoats or hoops. Her blond hair had been rinsed with a champagne pink tint and piled elaborately atop her head, pink ostrich plumes growing out of it. She looked like a character out of a Mae West movie with her dangling earrings and exposed cleavage, just a bit tawdry even with a fortune on her back. He ignored her and fiddled with the watch fob and chain looped across the front of his vest, er, waistcoat.

The moment Cassidy entered the building he knew it. Even before she stepped into the brightly tented and draped "ball-room" he was aware of her movements. She took his breath away. Her dark gold hair had been styled in a flattering Gibson Girl, the front a froth of curls, with two long tendrils left to cling lovingly to her neck in the back. She wore no adornment in it other than a black comb covered with jet beads. Her gown was made of a dark purple satin accented with black lace edging and tiny pink rosettes, the skirt gathered into an elaborate bustle of softly ruffled layers in the back. The long, leg-of-mutton sleeves tapered to points that extended past the bottom knuckles of the middle fingers of her hands, rendering gloves unnecessary. The tight wedding ring collar accented the graceful length of her neck. Tiny rosebuds clipped to her lobes called attention to the delicacy of her dainty ears. She could have walked off the pages of a history book and done justice to the name of Vanderbilt or Morgan, so much did she look her part. He walked straight past Betina and offered Cassidy his arm, exactly as a gentleman of nearly a century past would have done.

"You look marvelous!" she said, placing her hand on his forearm.

"You are simply beautiful," he told her, "inside and out."

She tilted back her head and laughed. Such a lovely sound! He covered her hand with his.

She was on his arm when the first guest arrived and thereafter for the majority of the remainder. He introduced her to everyone he knew. Before long, however, it became clear that someone else had laid the path for them. People began saying things like, "Ah, so this is the bright young consultant who planned this shindig!" and "I'm so impressed, Ms. Penno! Have you done many of these affairs?" It didn't take Paul long to figure out that Betina had stationed herself nearer the door outside the "tent" in order to be the first to greet their guests and explain Cassidy's presence by singing her praises as a hired consultant. Silently he conceded the point. The night, after all, was young.

He kept Cassidy with him during dinner, ignoring the place cards Betina had so painstakingly arranged. He gave himself free rein to enjoy her company, and soon found that she was the delight of everyone at the table, Hoot especially. Only Betina was not delighted, but she kept her displeasure well hidden behind a mask, which none but Paul recognized as a sham. She had scattered the family throughout the hall with instructions to sing Paul's praises and set their guests at ease. He resented that she used them for what amounted to business purposes but was relieved that no one seemed to object.

When the moment came for the cast members to take their positions backstage, Paul made a point of rising and excusing them both, finishing by saying warmly. "We're on, darling. Time to go."

Cassidy shot him a slightly startled glance, and Betina's smile slipped to a glower before she quickly disciplined it. Paul smiled at the babble of speculation he heard at their exit.

"They seem very much an item."

"Oh, no, I assure you, just friends."

"Looks like more than friendship to me."

"They make a charming couple, don't they?"

"It's rather an obligation. She's the sister of one of our most trusted employees."

"She's the love of his life," Paul whispered as he escorted her through the tables, his hand placed possessively in the small of her slender back.

"What are you up to?" she asked as soon as they were backstage.

"Just enjoying myself," he said casually. Then he smiled. "I can't help it when I'm with you."

They went their separate ways. As the announcement was made and the narration began, Cassidy exchanged her purple satin for a simple calico sacque, white apron and mob cap, while Paul stripped out of his cut-away, waistcoat and snowy shirt, then donned a red-and-white-striped one in its place, tied a kerchief about his neck and pushed up his sleeves and fixed them in place with garters before donning apron and cap. He was standing at a kitchen table, dusted in flour, his hands in real dough when the lights came up. She had her back to him, apron strings tied in a jaunty bow as she stirred a bubbling cooking pot on a massive cast-iron stove. She stopped occasionally to wipe imaginary sweat from her brow, and she and Paul glanced at each other, smiling, as the narrator told how Theo and Jane had sold baked goods from their own kitchen at first, giving up stable jobs in an established bakery to strike out on their own. Together they counted pennies, pondered bills and worked late into the night to make ends meet. The struggle was frightening, but Theo was determined and Jane ever supportive.

As the moment approached for the kiss, Paul hurried into it, obviously eager, and made a thorough job of it, sacrificing the poignancy of the moment for sheer ardor. Andy rushed to bring the narrative up to speed, Paul having jumped the gun on him, but the final words were lost in the roar of applause from an audience who had received a clear message. Cassidy

Penno was more than a hireling of any sort and more than a friend to the CEO of Barclay Bakeries.

As soon as the lights were down, Cassidy pulled out of his embrace, whispering urgently, "Paul, have you lost your mind?"

"No," he said. "In fact, I think I've found it."

"Will you tell me what is going on?"

"I won't marry her, Cass."

"How can you not?"

"I'll find a way."

"Even if it means giving up the company, breaking your word to your family and leaving them vulnerable?"

"Yes."

There wasn't time to say more as William hissed at them from offstage to get a move on. Time for another costume change, as well as a change of set. Paul yanked at his kerchief and followed Cassidy from the stage. He was beginning to feel the desperation of this final effort to save all. He realized that the chances of changing Betina's mind were not good, but his resolve never to marry her or anyone other than Cassidy only deepened, no matter what he had to do to make it happen. It wouldn't be easy to leave Barclay Bakeries, to confer his stock and his position on someone else, but he told himself that Cal would do a good job. He would protect the family's interest, perhaps as well as Paul himself.

A pang of deep loss assailed him, but he would not turn back now. Better to live with the loss of his life's work than the loss of the one woman who meant happiness itself to him. He was not, after all, Theo. Theo had had his bakery and his Jane, too. Paul would settle for the woman he loved. With what, he wondered, would he replace Barclay Bakeries? It was a question better pondered after the fact, one he would face later, with Cassidy at his side. If his heart pounded fit to fl from his chest, it was just in anticipation of the moment he could ask Cassidy Penno to be his wife. He wouldn't allow it to be anything else, and he would never look back. For Cass, for both their sakes, he would never look back.

Chapter Nine

The drama became a nightmare of endurance for Cassidy. She could not concentrate on the role of Jane and ponder how best to keep Paul from sabotaging himself. She felt helpless and frightened. When he met her backstage after the production, apparently jubilant over the rousing applause, she tried to put some distance between them by pleading that she had responsibilities to attend to. He said only that they should get changed quickly, and she hurried away to do just that, thinking that she might slip away before he could come for her. When she emerged from behind the curtain enclosing the women's dressing area, however, he was there, smiling and waiting. She tried to beg off.

"Paul, I really should check—"

"Whatever it is will take care of itself. The rest of this evening is ours to enjoy."

Only this evening, she told herself. *Only this one evening.* She nodded and allowed him to sweep her out onto the stage again where, together, to more applause, despite the fact that the band was playing, they descended a set of narrow steps to the floor below.

"No one's dancing," he said, though a few couples had taken to the floor. "Well, we'll see about that." Avoiding a surge of verbal congratulations with nods and smiles and clever footwork, he literally towed her by the hand through the tables and across the dance floor to the orchestra dais, where he spoke briefly with the saxophonist who doubled as conductor. In short order, the music came to a conclusion and the "conductor" stepped to the microphone to announce that the season's—that was the 1902 season's—most popular waltz was dedicated to the memory of Theo and Jane Barclay. A pointed gesture brought the lights down, and Paul hurried her to the center of the dance floor. A spotlight came on, searched the floor briefly and settled on Paul and Cassidy. In the second before the music began, Cassidy understood what he planned.

"Paul, I don't know how to waltz!" she whispered.

He seemed surprised, then he smiled. "Child's play," he assured her as the music began. "Just pick up your skirt and follow me."

She dipped and swept up her skirt. Paul's hands settled into place. "Forward in a straight line," he whispered, stepping off neatly. She managed to follow smoothly. "And now backward…and to the right…and all the way around." He smiled at her. "There, you see, together we can do anything."

Together. Her throat closed. Together was the one thing they could not be, whatever he might think at the moment. She lowered her eyes to hide the tears filling them. He pulled her a tad closer, and she bowed her head, giving herself up to this one last pleasure, this one last moment as a pair, a team.

After a few more bars the lights came up and couples flowed onto the dance floor, laughing and chatting. Cassidy stepped further into Paul's arms and clung to the illusion with all her might. When the waltz stretched to its inevitable ending, the band moved seamlessly into a bluesy rendition of a familiar folk song. Paul pulled her closer still, and they swayed to the music, her head on his shoulder. Song after song, they danced.

Paul ignored one attempt to cut in on him, sweeping her around the edge of the floor. Finally he glanced at his watch.

"An hour to the new year."

She was shocked. "So late?"

"Cass, it's not too late for us," he told her softly. "I won't let it be."

"But, Paul, what can you do without—"

"I want to talk to you!" The angry, determined voice took them both by surprise, so much so that they stopped in their tracks there at the edge of the dance floor. Betina glared at Paul, then moderated her expression for the benefit of those around her. Cassidy she ignored as insignificant. Cassidy gulped and made as if to move away, but Paul's arms instantly tightened.

"No. Whatever it is can wait."

Betina pushed in between them, though Paul kept a firm grip on Cassidy's hand. "No, it cannot wait!" she hissed. "You're trying to make a fool of me, and I won't stand for it!"

"Won't you?" Paul asked coolly. "And just what do you think you can do about it except to quit the field gracefully and resign yourself to the inevitable?"

"I'll ruin you!" Betina promised, no longer keeping her voice as low as necessary. Heads began to turn. Paul laughed mirthlessly.

"Don't be stupid."

"Your precious company—" she began, but Paul cut her off, making no effort at all to keep the conversation from reaching other ears.

"I'll resign. I will. What I won't do is marry you."

People around them began to stop and stare. Cassidy held her breath. He had to know how great a gamble he was taking. Betina glanced around them, and for a moment Cassidy thought that she would back down, at least delay the confrontation. Instead, she set her face grimly, squared her shoulders and lifted her chin. Her face twisted into a mask of pure venom. "How dare you use me like this!" she proclaimed loudly.

Cassidy's eyes widened with horror, but Paul merely bowed his head, smiling secretively. "I haven't used you, Betina," he said calmly, almost conversationally. "You walked into my office naked as the day you were born and threw yourself at my feet." Betina screamed and slapped him. His head jerked to one side. Calmly he turned back to face her and went on. "Much to my regret, we used each other for a time. But that's long over. I will not submit to your blackmail."

"Damn you!"

"Paul," Cassidy urged, gripping his wrist. "Not now. Please!"

"I won't marry you," he said to Betina, ignoring Cassidy. "I'll resign. I'll give away my Barclay shares. But I won't marry you."

It was as if the whole room came to standstill, despite the music playing gamely on. Whispers flew around the floor.

"Spencer's resigning."

"It's suicide, businesswise."

"Awful timing."

"Where are we without Spencer?"

"Square one."

"In the cellar!"

Suddenly William was at Paul's side, laughing stupidly and trying to smooth over what had become a much-too-public scene. "Now, now, kiddies. No public brawling. I suggest a time out."

"Go to hell, Penno!" Betina snarled. "If you'd taken your little slut of a sister out of my way as I'd asked you to—"

Paul's insouciance vanished. He took a threatening step forward. "Shut your mouth, or I'll shut it for you." Alarmed, William unwisely grabbed Paul by the arm.

Cassidy sent him a shocked, censorious glance before turn-

ing her attention fully to Paul. Whatever lengths she might
drive him to, Paul would never strike a woman. The way he
shook off William, proclaimed that he had no such scruples
where men were concerned, however, and Cassidy knew that
she had only seconds to avert true, and very public, disaster.
She pulled her hand free of his and stepped close. "Let it go,
Paul. She's trying to provoke you."

As if to prove her point, Betina threw back her head and
shrieked at Paul. "I'll bury your precious bakeries!"

"Even if I'm not there?"

"Especially if you're not there!"

"Then there's nothing to say."

Betina paused, glaring at him. "You'd give up everything?"

"Not everything," he said, "not Cassidy. Never Cassidy."

Horrified, Cassidy divided a desperate look between them.
They couldn't mean this! But they did. Betina looked down
her nose at Cass and smirked, eyes narrowing dangerously.
"Very well," she said. "Barclay Bakeries dies, and you get
your little playmate."

"No!" Cassidy backed away, shaking her head. She
couldn't let this happen. Not to Paul, not to his family. She
looked around her blindly. William stepped up to her side.
She shook him off, thinking only that he would never understand. Tony's face suddenly appeared from nowhere.
She moved toward it, desperately grateful. "Take me home!"
she whispered. To his credit Tony merely nodded and turned
her toward the door.

"Cassidy!" Paul clamped a hand on her shoulder turning
her back. "Don't go."

She turned away. "I have to."

"No! Sweetheart, wait." He put himself in her path, seized
both her hands.

"Get out of her way, Spencer."

Paul ignored Tony as if he didn't exist. "Stay with me,

Cass. We'll bring in the new year together, the way it should be.''

She shook her head, splintering inside. "I-I can't. Betina—''

He stepped close, bending his head. "She doesn't mean it! She'd be cutting her own throat, destroying her own income!''

"It doesn't matter," she whispered, desperate to get away before he could convince her to let him sacrifice himself. She wanted to tell him that she wouldn't let him do it. He couldn't give up everything he'd worked so hard to build, not now when all his hard work was about to come to fruition. She couldn't be the cause of that. She needed to tell him, but the words lodged in her throat, trapped by the tears that threatened to spill down her cheeks. Tony hovered at her elbow. She grabbed him and held on. Doggedly he pushed her through the crowd and tables. Paul kept pace until they reached the edge of the tent. She knew that he spoke, but she couldn't hear the words for the misery roaring in her brain. Once free of the tent, she ran, Tony beside her. At some point, she realized Paul was no longer following. It was then that she began to sob, then that Tony took her in his arms and held her. Then that the loss finally broke her and she let it sweep her away.

Paul stood in the dark of his office, brooding. What a fiasco, Betina ranting at him like a madwoman, Cassidy running away, William bleating one inane comment after another in a vain attempt to cover what could never be hidden. Paul had pulled himself together and made a dignified public apology devoid of explanation, then quietly exited. He had intended to go after Cassidy at once, but reason told him that it was wiser to wait. Better to do what he now knew had to be done and then present her with a *fait accompli*. Otherwise, she would try to talk him out of it. She would see herself as responsible for his losses, when Betina was really to blame. He couldn't let that happen, so he would do what had to be done and go to her afterward.

He turned into the room, the heavy glass of the window cool against his back, and slipped his hands into the pockets of his pants. Carefully, a bit at a time, he looked around the room. This paneled office had once been his grandfather's. Betina had tried to get him to paint the golden oak paneling white and replace the burgundy and gold carpet with pale gray. She had envisioned a glass and chrome desk and Danish modern chairs. Paul had laughed at her, and she had taken immediate offense, but he could find no reason not to love this room just as it was. He tried to envision how Cassidy would decorate it and chuckled at a vision of Tiffany lamp shades, glowing candles, and paisley prints. Suddenly he felt her absence with keen longing. He was not complete when she was away from him. As hard as it would be to leave this room for the final time, it would be much, much more difficult, even unbearable, to give up Cassidy.

He crossed over to his desk, clicked on the banker's lamp that sat to one side pulled out the chair and sat down. Carefully he opened the center drawer and selected a pen, laid it beside the blotter and closed the drawer. Turning slightly to one side, he opened another drawer and extracted a single sheet of company stationery, which he placed in the very center of the desk blotter and smoothed needlessly with his hand. Sitting forward in his chair, he checked the pocket watch that had once belonged to Theo. Three minutes past midnight. He picked up the pen and wrote the date at the top of the paper. January 1. What a way to start the new year. He shook his head, took a deep breath, then began to write. When he had finished, some minutes later, he lifted the paper and read aloud what he had written:

"To whom it may concern:
It has been my pleasure and my privilege to serve this

company and the family it represents in one position or another, from errand boy to CEO, for more than twenty years. During that time, I have sought to perform my duties to the very best of my abilities. Had I been as scrupulous about my private life, I would not now find it necessary to tender my resignation, effective immediately. My final act, if it is permissible, is to recommend Cal Thomas as my replacement. I believe that Cal will tend the family till, so to speak, with the same care and skill as I myself. My gratitude is extended to many persons too numerous to mention here. Let me say then, in conclusion, that I wish only the best for this company and the noble family who are its shareholders.

Sincerely, Paul Barclay Spencer."

Well, that about said it all. He let out a sigh and rubbed a twitching muscle in the hollow of one temple with the tip of his forefinger. Then he folded the letter in thirds, creasing it sharply twice with the edge of his thumbnail. He took out an envelope, slipped the letter into it and folded down the flap before tucking it into the breast pocket of his rented coat. That done, he reached for the telephone and dialed the first of five numbers, each of which he knew by heart. As expected, he reached only answering machines. None of the residents would be home yet. They were all at the party, all except perhaps Betina. He left the same message on every machine. He was calling an urgent meeting for one o'clock that afternoon at the Thomases'. He apologized to Joyce and Cal for appropriating their home but promised that he would explain as soon as he saw them.

After he hung up from the final call, he sat for several moments longer, letting the ambience, the history, of this place fill him one last time. Then he switched off the lamp, got up, and fished his keys out of his pocket. He removed the ring that held keys to the building and laid it in the center of the blotter.

As he rode the elevator down and walked through the lobby he thought about all the improvements that had been made over the years. He remembered how they'd grown, flourished really, and felt a sense of pride in all that had been accomplished. His contributions had been many. He could be proud of that, at least. Hereafter, he meant to live his life, personally as well as professionally, in a manner in which he could always take pride. For that he could thank Cassidy, that and so much else.

He walked out of the building and went home, where he turned off the telephones, boxed his costume for return, took a shower and tried to catch a few hours sleep. He was more successful than he'd expected. Waking about ten, he shaved, dressed, put the costume box in the car and went out for a late breakfast. The city had apparently partied hard the night before, for the streets were all but deserted in the light of day.

Paul thought of Cassidy. Had she slept as well as he? Was she able to enjoy her breakfast. Did she have the hope that he would work things out so they could be together? Did she even understand how much he loved her? He didn't see how she could. After all, she had offered him her most precious gift, her virginity, and he had walked away from it, but surely she knew how difficult that had been for him. Surely she had felt the strength of his love last night. If not, he would see to it that she understood—just as soon as he got through this meeting. He knew that though the shop would officially be closed today, she would be receiving returned costumes from last night's party between one and four. He wanted to be at the shop before four.

He took his time over breakfast, then drove around for a while, washed the car, checked all the fluids and the pressure in the tires and filled the gas tank. When he'd killed enough time, he drove to his cousin's house, arriving around half past

noon. Joyce answered the door wearing pink fleece and bedroom slippers. Because she wore no cosmetics, he easily iden-
ified the slightly purplish half-moons shadowing her eyes.

He leaned forward and kissed her cheek, which she turned
up for him. "Hey, cuz. You feeling okay? Baby giving you a
little morning sickness?"

She shook her head, dark ponytail swinging. "Nope. I'm
fine. Just a little tired." She turned and led him through the
impressive, vaulted entry into the spacious living room, saying, "Late night last night."

He nodded a little shamefacedly. "Party break up late?"

She sent him an enigmatic look. "Not particularly. Cal and
left right after the 'Auld Lang Syne.'"

"I see."

"We missed you," she said lightly.

He looked away, muttering, "I sort of lost my party mood."

Joyce waited until he looked at her again before saying
gently, "You love her very much, don't you, your Miss
Penno."

He smiled. "Very much."

"I'm glad. Sit down. I'll get Cal."

He wandered toward the massive sofa in the center of the
room, but bypassed it and went instead to the low-backed armchair placed close to the free-standing rock fireplace that divided the living area from the dining area. Joyce had been
gone only moments when the doorbell rang. Just as Paul began
to wonder if he should go and answer it, the door opened and
his aunt Mary's voice rang out, "Yoo-hoo! Joyce dear, it's
Mother!"

He stood and called to her. "In here, Aunt Mary."

Presently Mary appeared, wearing a simple gray wool skirt,
walking shoes and a red sweater embroidered all over with
"Happy New Year!" in what appeared to be every known
language. She wore a red headband and looked rather girlish
for it, her thick white hair waving about her face in untutored

curls. The thought struck Paul that she had not taken time to style her hair, and as she drew nearer, he noticed something odd about her lipstick. It feathered at the edges, accentuating unkindly the small wrinkles around her mouth. His own lips twitched as he faced the sudden knowledge that his dear aunt, sweet little lady that she was, had been wearing carefully applied lip liner lo these many years and he had failed to notice. She was a woman, he realized, like any other. The thought fascinated. He began to count in his head the number of years that she had been a widow.

Joyce and Cal arrived then. It seemed that Paul had gotten his entire family out of bed for this meeting, an impression confirmed by Uncle John shambling in a quarter hour later, his hoary jaw unshaven, his voice still rough and thick from sleep. He had hardly rumbled a hello when Joyce got up to fetch coffee, and the entire party, save Paul, heaved a sigh of relief for needs about to be met. He could only chuckle as the steaming mugs were passed to eager hands.

"The party must have improved considerably after I left," he commented only half-teasingly. "You all look as though you were up until the wee hours." Was it his imagination, or did an expression of conspiratorial guilt tiptoe around the room. He opened his mouth to ask what was going on, but John beat him to it.

"All right, Paul, out with it."

Again he opened his mouth. Again he was forestalled. "We agreed to wait for everyone to arrive, John," Cal said, the ring of authority in his voice.

John grunted, and before Paul could ask when they had made such an agreement, Mary said rather forcefully, "I enjoyed last night's dramatic presentation, Paul. I would say that was one of your better ideas, and you were really quite good, you and Miss Penno."

"Penno," John rumbled. "Kin to that what's-his-name, is she?"

"William," Paul confirmed.

"Never cared for him," John stated flatly.

"She's his sister."

"Which is not to say, of course, that I would not like Miss Penno herself. I'm not one to judge too quickly, as you know, and after all, what would an old bachelor like me know about young women? I merely said that I do not care for the brother. Something of a toad, don't you think? Er, the brother, mind, not the sister."

Paul was flabbergasted and mildly amused. "I, ah, am persuaded, Uncle John, that you will like Cassidy quite well."

"Just as I suspected," John muttered. "Just as I suspected."

"She is not at all like—"

The doorbell chimed, and Joyce leaped to her feet. "That will be Uncle Carl and Aunt Jewel. I'll just let them in. The help is off for the holiday, you know, not that it matters, Paul, not that it matters at all."

"William." Paul finished, watching her hurry from the room as if escaping some peril unknown to him. The notion was so strong that he actually looked all around him, twisting about in his chair to do so, the others studiously ignoring him. What was going on here? Would eerie music start to play next, like it did in the movies to warn an unsuspecting audience that it should prepare to scream?

Carl and Jewel entered the room shepherded by Joyce. If anything, this pair looked even worse for wear than the motley crew already assembled. Carl was as bleary-eyed as if he had not slept at all. His clothing, on the other hand, might have been slept in. Jewel wore no cosmetics at all, her silver blond hair scraped back into a tight twist at the nape of her neck. He rose as Jewel came straight across the room toward him. To his surprise and confusion, despite the tense look in her eyes, she merely laid a hand upon his shoulder. From sheer habit, he bent forward, and she kissed him on the cheek, her hand patting him understandingly.

Carl took a seat on the sofa next to Cal. Jewel perched on the edge next to him. Cal sent a pointed look at Carl, who shook his head meaningfully. At once Cal said, "Let's begin." Betina, apparently, would not be in attendance. So be it. Paul took the letter from his pocket and carried it to John, who extracted the single sheet from the envelope and quickly scanned its contents. Silently he passed the letter over to Carl, who read it with Jewel peeking openly over his shoulder. The letter then moved to Cal, who merely glanced at it and passed it on to Joyce. Paul waited uncomfortably while Joyce carefully read every word. When she came to the part about Cal being recommended to assume Paul's vacated post, she elbowed her husband and silently pointed it out. Cal folded his arms and shook his head, as if to say the idea was without merit. Joyce passed the letter to her mother, who read the whole with sad eyes. When she was done she leaned forward and laid it upon Paul's knee. He didn't want it back. He folded it and laid in on the coffee table, a huge glass and wrought-iron affair with rough corners.

Paul got up, unnerved by the silence, and clasped his hands behind his back. Perhaps they were waiting for explanation. He cleared his throat. "Last year," he began, "before Grand-father died, I allowed myself to be seduced into an affair both unsavory and unwise..."

"We heard," said John baldly, "that she came to you and presented herself naked as a jaybird."

Paul's jaw dropped. For a long moment he could only stare. Heat clogged his throat. He coughed it away. "Uh, I may have said things last night in anger and desperation that would have been better left unsaid. I apologize, to you especially, Aunt Jewel, and I promise—"

"Oh, she admitted it," Jewel said dismissively.

"A-admitted..."

"We feel," said Aunt Mary, "that Betina may be in need of some professional counseling."

"She won't go, of course," Carl stated flatly. "That girl is too willful by half, and I blame myself. I really do."

"Yourself, Uncle Carl?"

"In my zeal," Carl went on, "to make her feel one of the family, I fear I overlooked behavior and attitudes that I should have corrected."

"I am more to blame," Jewel said. "As her natural parent, I should have taken the lead in discipline, but she never listened to me, you see, and it was so much easier to let Carl deal with it in his quiet, sensible fashion."

"It might have been different if her natural father had allowed me to adopt her as I wished to do," Carl said. "Heaven knows he took no particular interest in the child and contributed nothing to her support, but he remained adamant on that one point."

"I had hoped," said Jewel, "that love would change her, soften her somehow, cure her of the need to demand and manipulate. I was foolish, trying to see what was not there between you."

"Poor Father thought her a sad, empty-headed sort of child," Carl said. "I'm sure he felt that she needed someone to look after her, and no doubt she professed undying love for you, my boy."

"And," said John, "there was his fear that you would choose my path and fail to marry."

Paul felt overwhelmed. "I see. I assume that you have had a chance to speak with her then."

"Oh, we had a meeting," Joyce said, "last night."

"And we made some decisions," said Cal.

For a long moment Paul could only stare. No wonder they were so tired and disheveled. After the party, they had called a meeting of their own! Paul rubbed a hand over the back of his neck and sat down in his chair. Somehow he had lost control of his meeting. He wasn't even certain, at the moment,

what was going on! Cal enlightened him. "Your resignation
is rejected."

Paul sprang to the edge of his chair. "That's very kind of
you, but, Cal, you of all people know that I can't—"

"Of course you can," Mary interrupted. "It's all very simple, really."

"I don't understand."

"Ah, perhaps this will help," Uncle John said, leaning forward to extract from his back pocket a folded sheet of paper,
which he tossed onto the coffee table.

"And this," said Mary, extracting a similar paper from her
small handbag.

"And this," said Joyce, snatching from Cal the paper that
suddenly appeared in his hand.

"And, of course," began Carl, producing his own paper,
which he handed to his wife.

"This," said Jewel, adding it to the pile on the table.

Paul stared at the little heap of folded papers. Carefully he
leaned far forward and picked up the one on top. Flicking it
open, he stared, dumbfounded, at the bill of sale making over
to him, for the amount of one dollar, Carl's—and thereby
Jewel's— share of Barclay Bakeries. He knew without having
to look that all the other papers as good as handed over to him
the remaining shares, save, of course, Betina's thirty percent.
The enormity of what they had done hit him like a ton of
brick. They had handed him their livelihoods without the least
reservation!

"I-I cannot accept this."

"You must," said Mary.

"We thought first," Joyce explained, "that we would simply activate our respective positions on the board and stand
with you, as a block."

"But then," said Jewel, "I realized that I am vulnerable to
Betina's schemes. I wouldn't want to take the risk of letting
my judgment be clouded."

"We thought it best," said John, "simply to put the matter entirely in your hands."

"To give you the power to control her," Cal stated decisively.

"B-but it's your only income!"

"Oh, we still expect to be paid," Mary said.

"But you haven't guaranteed that will happen! You can't just hand it over blindly!"

"And why not?" John asked. "We've trusted you implicitly all these years to take care of us. Why should that change now? This way, you see, there can be no question about who is in charge. Betina cannot doubt that you have the power and the will to fight her."

"And if it makes you feel better," Cal said, "we'll draw up something later spelling out your obligations to each of us."

Paul stared at the man who could have had his job and marveled. He looked at Joyce, her face shining, at Mary, content and unruffled, at John, placid and unconcerned. He looked at Carl and Jewel and saw regret—and trust. Gently he eased back in his chair. He swallowed and tried to speak, but where were the words to express what he was feeling? How did one respond to such overwhelming love, such absolute trust? After several minutes John got up, stretched, and scratched his head.

"Well, I'm off. Think I'll take a nap. Dining with friends later. Good day all."

Jewel and Carl were rising before he'd finished speaking. "We didn't sleep much last night," she said. "Frankly, I'd like a long hot bath and a glass of wine, but I suppose I really ought to eat something first."

"I'll do you an omelet or something," Carl said. "Better yet, we can pick up something on the way home."

"Marvelous idea!"

They went out discussing what to pick up to eat. Mary got up, too. "Joyce dear, I want you to go back to bed."

Cal waggled an eyebrow, leering. "And you wonder why I adore your mother," he said to Joyce, who laughed. Mary took a playful swat at him and trundled toward the door.

"Paul, I'll see you soon. Bring your lovely Miss Penno, will you, dear? I look forward to a closer acquaintance. Happy New Year!"

Cal got up and stretched without seeming in the least weary. "Think I'd better have a quick shave," he said. He bent and kissed his wife on the mouth. "Don't be long."

Joyce shook her head, grinning. "We're awful, I know," she said to Paul, "but we've tried so long, and now that I'm pregnant, well, it just sort of takes the 'work' out of it, you know?"

Paul made no reply other than a slightly embarrassed smile. Joyce got up and walked toward him. She bent down to bring her face on a level with his and looped an arm loosely about his neck. "I'm so happy for you. And I want you to know, we all understand that for our sakes you'd have married that scheming Betina without a word of complaint to any of us, if not for Miss Cassidy Penno. For that alone, we're bound to love her. And one more thing. Cal won't say it, but I will. It means a great deal to both of us that you would recommend him to take your place, but frankly, I'm glad he won't have to. It's a great burden to bear, the welfare of so many people, and I don't just mean the family. You were bred to it. It's yours by right, and so is the woman you love." She placed a kiss just to the side of his mouth and said, "Now I suggest you go get her."

It was the least necessary piece of advice he'd ever received, but welcome, nonetheless.

He stood and looked down at her. "Thanks, cuz. You called last night's meeting, didn't you?" She merely grinned, her hands clasped behind her back. "Did Betina really admit to that stunt she pulled in my office?"

"Betina has a way of letting her temper get the better of

her," Joyce said. "She not only admitted doing you the high honor of seducing you, she ranted about how you insulted her by wanting out later. She said—quite authoritatively, I might add—that was the best sex you'd ever had."

"Ha! Shows how much she knows! The best sex I've ever had I didn't even get!" At Joyce's look of intrigued puzzlement, he merely smiled secretively, waved a hand and said, "Never mind."

"Uh-huh, well, anyway, she scandalized the old folk, and when she started raving about burying the Bakeries just to get at you, everyone knew we had to do something. We discussed it and discussed it, and Cal finally came up with the ironclad solution. Not a soul objected, Paul."

"I'll never forget it," he vowed, "and I'll never let down you or any of the family."

"We never doubt it. Now go, will you?"

He laughed and said, "I'll let myself out." He was still chuckling when he got in his car.

Chapter Ten

Cassidy sighed and looked at the green plumed hat as if she had never before seen it. She had intended, several minutes ago, to box it with the costume with which it belonged, but thoughts of Paul and last night's very public scene had distracted her. She still remembered in agonizing detail the look of utter malice on Betina's twisted face—and all because of her. She shuddered to think that she, however unwittingly, had brought that down on Paul. How could he think she would let him lose everything for her? She shook her head, uncertain with whom she was angriest, Paul or *that woman*.

Tony was in the front, receiving the returned costumes, inspecting them for damage, and carrying them back to Cassidy for repair, if needed, and proper packaging for shipping to the consignor. She had reglued the feather on the hat after inserting a tiny wire into the broken stem in order to stiffen it. She now wrapped it carefully in plastic and placed it within the reinforced niche inside the box. As she worked, she heard Tony speaking with someone out front. Nothing remarkable about that. They'd been coming in steadily for the past two hours, returning their costumes and gushing. Some of them wanted to gossip about the scene between Paul and Betina, but Tony showed surprising adeptness in avoiding the subject. Cassidy was surprised then when she realized that he had raised his voice almost angrily—until she recognized the answering voice as Paul's.

She closed her eyes. She had been dreading this moment since she'd found herself in Tony's car the night before and realized that she had merely put off the final confrontation. Eventually she would have to convince Paul beyond any doubt that it was over between them, irrevocably, completely over. She had searched her heart and her mind for hours for a way to do that, knowing that no matter what her words, he was likely to see the truth on her face or in her eyes. She would be surprised if he couldn't *feel* it in the air, for it seemed at times that their bodies sent these invisible, uncontrollable messages to each other. Yet she was determined. She could not let him give up everything for which he'd worked for so much of his life. For the first time, she truly understood how he could walk away from her that night when she'd meant to seduce him. He had believed it best for her. Now she had to do what was best for him.

She wasn't surprised when he pushed his way into the workroom, Tony with him. "I told him you didn't want to see him," Tony grumbled. "He wouldn't listen. As usual."

Paul threw off Tony's hands with a shrugging motion of his shoulders and arms. Tony bristled, looking rather like a puppy playing attack dog. Paul ignored him with insulting ease, saying to Cassidy, "I have to talk to you."

She kept doing what she was doing, fastening the straps attached to the costume box containing the green hat. "Paul, we said all we had to say to each other some time ago." She flicked a glance up at him. "You said it yourself. You're not the man for me."

"Things have changed."

"Not as far as I'm concerned."

"Honey, please listen to me. I'm not giving up anything to be with you. My family has—"

"That's what you say now," she cut in. "That's not what you said the last time."

"Last night—"

"Not last night, Paul, *last time*. You said, quite clearly, that you are not the man for me. I've decided you're right."

"That was before I realized that I just couldn't give you up! And it was before—"

"She said she isn't interested, Spencer." Tony stepped forward, puffing out his chest in a show of aggression. "What's it take for you to get it, a building to fall on your head? The lady's moved on, see?"

"No, I don't see, and if you don't get out of my face, you little twit, I'm gonna smack you!"

"That's it," Cassidy said, getting up from her work table to walk over to the wall-mounted phone. "I'm calling the police." She lifted the receiver.

"You're what?"

She turned back to face him, the receiver pressed against her ear. "I said if you don't leave, I'm going to call the police."

"Are you out of your mind? I only want to talk to you, to explain—"

Cassidy turned back to the phone and pretended to punch in the three-digit emergency number. In the process, she caught Tony's eye and gave him an almost imperceptible nod. As prearranged, Tony delivered the *coup de grace*.

"Don't you get it?" he shouted practically in Paul's face. "Cassidy's made her choice. She spent last night with *me*."

A shocked silence told her that Tony's words had had the desired effect. She closed her eyes and bit her lip, knowing that she had to get him out of there quickly before she herself broke down and admitted that she'd only spent the night on

Tony's couch, crying, in case Paul had gone looking for her at her house. Calling up more strength than she'd known she possessed, she turned back to face Paul, trying not to see his stricken expression, and said very clearly into the telephone receiver, "I want to report a belligerent customer at my shop at—" She didn't have to say more. Paul turned and walked out of the building without another word.

He was in shock. He sat in his living room, staring at the empty fire grate and the pine cones mixed in among the poinsettias that his housekeeper had arranged around it. The decorated tree in the corner was dark and cold, which was just how he felt. Tony. He'd known, of course, from the very beginning that the boy—and he was a *boy*—had a crush on Cassidy, but Cass herself had been aware and unimpressed. Well then, he had undoubtedly driven her to it. He had driven her straight into Tony's arms. Or had he?

He sat forward on the dark green leather sofa and clasped his hands together. She had been uncomfortable last night with all the attention he was showering on her, the public attention, anyway. Privately, she'd always been so wonderfully responsive, so warm and loving and so magically right. She was twenty-five years old. For twenty-five years she had waited for the right man with whom to share herself, and she had chosen him, not Tony. Out of sheer love, he had refused to accept such a magical, treasured gift, but nothing had ever meant more to him than the offering. Had his refusal driven her to Tony? Not right away apparently. If at all.

A sudden certainty lanced through him, propelling him to his feet. No. Not Cassidy, not his loving, charming, so quietly strong Cassidy. What then was going on? Aw, God. He closed his eyes, feeling the strength of unselfish love wrap itself around him. He should have known instantly. He'd done it himself, made the hard choice, done what he was sure was best for her. Now she was doing what she thought was best for him. And he hadn't managed to tell her that the threat no longer existed. True, she hadn't given him much chance. Calling the police, for pity's sake! He could almost laugh. First, though, he had to find a way to make her listen to him.

And if he was wrong? If by some unimaginable irony she had actually done the thing she claimed to have done? Could he live with that?

He pushed his hands over his face, searching—and could find only one answer. He could not live without her. He could forgive her anything, at least once, for the chance to make a life with her. Now how to make her understand? How to get a hearing? Maybe he needed someone else to deliver the message, but to whom would she listen? Who was most likely to get a hearing even on an unhappy subject? And then he knew.

It was 3:40 when the rush hit. They'd received returns steadily all afternoon, and then suddenly they were swamped. Cassidy left the work room to help Tony, knowing that she'd have to finish repairs and packaging over the following days. They had planned for this. She knew what she was doing, and things would have been fine, if William and, incredibly, Betina Lincoln hadn't stormed in together. Cassidy could hardly believe her eyes, William bringing *that woman* here? Despite the fact that the shop was filled with people, Cassidy stopped what she was doing and came around the end of the counter. She stared at William, seeing only the same censure and disdain that she'd always seen, and she was in no mood to put up with it. She pointed at the door and said, "Get out."

Determination firmed William's face, and he stepped closer, grabbing her arm and spinning her about. "Not until I've had a few choice words with you, sister dear."

She wrenched her arm from his grip and glared over his shoulder at Betina, who had the sensitivity to look uncomfortable as those in the shop stared avidly. "How dare you bring her here?"

"Let's find a little privacy, and I'll explain it to you."

"Not now, or can't you see that I'm busy?"

"This can't wait."

Seizing her arm once more, he propelled her toward the next room, at the same time signaling Betina with a jerk of his head to follow them. They were barely inside when Tony appeared, eyeing Cassidy anxiously. "Want me to call someone? The police maybe?"

Cassidy grimaced. She'd threatened Paul with the police, but that had been an act, and William *was* her brother. Better just to get it over with so she could take care of business. No doubt once she'd told them what they wanted to hear—that hereafter she wouldn't be seeing Paul for any reason—they'd go away and leave her alone. Then she could get on with her life. Somehow. She lifted her chin and shook her head at Tony. "Just take care of the customers."

He looked doubtful, glancing at each of her visitors with as much curiosity as concern. "If you need anything..."

She bowed her head dismissingly. "Thank you."

He hesitated a moment longer and then withdrew. Cassidy turned to her companions and found her brother engaged in a meaningful look with Betina Lincoln. After a mere second or so, Betina pulled her gaze from William's and targeted Cassidy.

"You've ruined my life," she said, taking a casual step forward. She looked very cool and elegant today in slender gold knit slacks and matching turtleneck worn beneath a chocolate brown jacket with suede lapels. She did not look like a woman whose life had been ruined, not even like a woman whose life *could* be ruined.

Cassidy shook her head. "I haven't done anything to you."

"How can you say that?" Betina countered. "You've taken from me the only man I've ever wanted."

Wanted, not loved. Cassidy smiled at the choice of wording, wondering if Betina even realized how easily she gave herself away. She folded her arms and cocked her head. "I feel sorry for you," she said, "not for the reasons you think, but I do pity you."

Betina sent a confused look at William, who instantly leaped to her assistance. "It's true, Cass. Paul degraded and debased her, and she let him because she loves him, and then he tossed her out. Just when things were beginning to work out for them, you entered the picture." He put a hand to his chest, humbly saying, "I take full responsibility for that. Knowing how...*impressionable* you are, I shouldn't have led him straight to you as I did. I just never dreamed he'd be so unscrupulous—or you so foolish." He glanced up sheepishly, adding, "I did warn you. I told you all about his situation."

Well, this was rich. Cassidy could almost laugh. She let her hands fall at her sides, then brought them to her hips, striking a cryptic pose. "Paul is not the sort to abuse or debase women. He's a decent, caring, honorable man—"

"He used me for sex!" Betina exclaimed.

"Oh, please. You used sex to try to trap him. He was human enough to play along, for a bit, but then he became ashamed and sickened, and he broke it off."

"How dare you?" Betina snapped, advancing closer, her hands knotted into fists.

William neatly intervened, stepping between them and saying hastily, "How honorable is a man who breaks his vows?"

"Vows?" Cassidy echoed. "What are you talking about?"

"He brought in the family," Betina informed her hotly. "After swearing not to, he bullied them into banding against me!"

"It's true!" William insisted. "All the years I've worked for Barclay's I've heard about that vow. He made a public pledge! He signed papers! Then, after promising to make things right with Betina, he went against everything and convinced the family to become involved. Betina's own parents were told vile things about her in order to win their compliance! You can't let it happen, Cassidy. If not for Betina then for yourself! How could you ever trust him after this? How could you live with him knowing what he's done?''

"You're insane," Cassidy said slowly. "Both of you. I don't know what's happened, but I do know that Paul would never break his vow. He couldn't live with that. He'd resign first.''

"That's what he wanted you to believe!" Betina insisted. "He'd say or do anything to get what he wants, anything!''

"Then why would you want him?" Cassidy countered. "Answer me that, if you can. If Paul's so awful, why have you gone to such ludicrous lengths to force him into marriage?''

For a moment Betina's mouth worked like that of a fish, oxygen going in but no sound coming out. Finally she thrust an impatient look at William and grated out, "Say something! Convince her!''

William took a deep breath. "Sh-she loves him anyway.''

Cassidy rolled her eyes. "They owe her, Cassidy! The whole family owe her! All her life they've denied her the s-social prominence a-and position to which she's entitled! She's had no say in her own life, no control, not socially, not financially, not in any real way.''

"All because I'm not a Barclay by blood!" Betina fumed. "You don't know what it's like being the odd man out, the different one. They could've adopted me, made me their own, but my stepfather wouldn't hear of it. They wouldn't even let me forget my accident of birth. They *made* me maintain contact with my real father, no matter that it shamed me. I didn't even want people to know that I was connected to that nothing, that nobody!''

"You can understand how it is, Cass!" William said urgently. "How many times have our own parents shamed and appalled us? Haven't you ever thought how different our lives might be if not for the accident of our births? We never had a real chance to be anything, but Betina does, and they won't let her take it! Don't you see?''

"My God,'' Cassidy breathed. They truly were obsessed, both of them, and their mutual obsession had drawn them together, not in love, not even in affection, but in greed and pride, to plot and scheme against what they saw as an unfair world. William, oh, William! To think of the guilt she'd borne for his shame, his obsession. He had heaped that guilt on her himself—and she had let him. "It's true,'' she whispered. "It's true!''

William sent Betina a triumphant look. "You'll do it then?'' he said, rushing at Cassidy to seize her by the upper arms. She flinched and tried to draw away. "You'll do it?''

"D-do what?''

"You'll tell Paul that you want no part of him. Make him understand that you want no part. And tell him why, make certain he understands that it's his lack of honor you cannot accept, that his refusal to do the right thing has ruined him in your eyes.'' He shook her then, pleading, "Will you do that, Cassidy? Will you help us right this terrible wrong? You're our only hope now. Make me proud of you for once, little sister! Do this one thing for me!''

One thing? As if she hadn't done hundreds, millions of *things* to try to win some small measure of regard from him. She began to understand finally, not just about William, not just about herself and William, but about Paul and what he had been trying to tell her earlier.

"I think I see it now,'' she said. "He's found a way to free himself, hasn't he? He's managed to get free of your schemes, and you need me to hook him for you again! You want me to shame him into doing what you want.'' She had to laugh then. It was either laugh or scream. "You don't know, do you? You don't know that I've already done what you want!'' Tears filled her eyes as she stared at her brother. "Oh, I am a fool,'' she whispered. "You're right about that. For me, he was willing to give up everything you covet so desperately, his business, his career, even his family's trust and regard. For me. But I couldn't let him. I'm not worth that, you see. You taught me that, William. You taught me that! And because of it, I turned him away this afternoon!"

William paled. "When?" He shook her again, roughly this time. "What time was it? Tell me!"

She shook her head, trying to clear it. "T-two. Around two."

William released her as suddenly as if she'd burned him, his gaze going to Betina. "Before he called me. *Before* he called me!"

Betina put her hands to her head, her eyes gone wild. "What do we do now? What do we do now?"

"Nothing."

Cassidy spun around to find Paul standing in the doorway, Tony peering over his shoulder. Her knees went weak, and she stumbled toward him. He took one step and swept her hard against him, his arm locking her to his chest.

"Paul!"

"It's all right, sweetheart. It's all right. You were right. We are free of them. Not in the way you think, but free, nonetheless. I would have resigned. I even wrote the letter and gave it to the family. It was the only solution I could live with, but it wasn't necessary. My family, you see, are as devoted to me as I to them. Once they understood that it's you I love, they took action of their own." He lifted his gaze to spear Betina. "They gave me their shares. I now control seventy percent of all Barclay stock. Betina has no power over me or the company."

"No!" Betina screamed. "No, they wouldn't!"

"Oh, but they did," Paul told her calmly.

"Because they know they can trust him," Cassidy supplied, pulling away from him to turn back to the others. "They know, as I know, that he would never do the things you accuse him of."

He brought his hands up to her shoulders and squeezed gently, pulling her back against him. "I'm not proud of some of the things I've done," he said, "but I would never break my word to my family. That's why I couldn't ask them for help. It never occurred to me that they would step in of their own free will, though it should have. They're like that, quiet, careful, a little restrained, I suppose, but their love, their support, is total."

"For you, maybe," Betina muttered hatefully. Real tears flowed from her eyes and stained her cheeks. "They never loved or supported me!"

"Of course they did," he told her, sighing. "It never made a moment's difference to them what your last name was. You only got away with this nonsense as long as you did because of their readiness to claim and support you. But love and acceptance was never enough for you. What you want is complete control over the family, the business, everything, and you thought you could do it by controlling me. But control is not the key. The key is responsibility. They trust me because I am willing to shoulder the responsibility of fulfilling their trust, just as Cassidy has been willing, for so long, to be bullied and belittled by her own brother in an attempt to keep peace in the family."

"That's why we are the strong ones," Cassidy said softly, placing her hand over his and looking back over her shoulder at him. She understood that William was weak despite his bluster and criticism, just as Betina was weak despite the schemes and threats and tantrums. Now she was beginning to realize that she was strong, strong enough to do what was best for those she loved whatever the cost to her. That was a lesson Paul had taught her, one of many.

"That's it," Paul said after a long, silent moment. "It's all over. I suggest you both vacate the premises immediately. Otherwise Tony will call the police. Won't you, Tony?''

Cassidy had forgotten about her young clerk's presence. She twisted to one side and looked around Paul to find him leaning against the wall with arms folded. "Won't you, Tony?''

He glowered for a moment, but then he pushed away from the wall and nodded, a smile hitching up one corner of his mouth. "Sure. Whatever you say.''

Cassidy smiled at him. "Thank you, Tony, for everything.''

He glanced at his feet almost shyly. Then he puffed out his chest, folded his arms and said with surprising force and authority, "All right, you two, out you go! No backtalk now. I'm just a step away from that phone.''

Betina looked for a moment as if she would pitch another of her infamous fits, but then she seemed to realize the futility of such an effort. With a glare of pure hatred, she swept past them and stalked out of the room. A moment later they heard the door to the sidewalk slam. William cleared his throat. "Cassidy, I'm, uh…''

Cassidy sighed. "Go away, William. I really don't want to be around you right now.''

His mouth thinned, and he nodded. "Perhaps later you'll feel more reasonable.''

"Cass is the soul of reason," Paul told him. "I, on the other hand, am not feeling particularly reasonable where you are concerned at the moment. I suggest you spend the holiday break getting your résumé in order. I don't think we'll be able to use you any longer at Barclay Bakeries.''

Cassidy was sorry to hear it, but she said nothing, merely bowing her head in acceptance. She understood that Paul could no longer trust William, even if William did not. His look of incredulity turned bitter, and he lashed out, as he always had, at her.

"I knew this would happen! I knew you'd cost me my job!''

"On the contrary," Paul said firmly. "I'd have fired you some time ago if not for your sister. I could overlook your condescending behavior toward me so long as you performed your job well, but your treatment of your own sister was enough to convince me that you are not the sort of individual I want for an employee. Nevertheless, I continued to tolerate you because of her concern for you and my respect for her judgment. No longer. You are finished at Barclay Bakeries."

"You promised!" William reminded Cassidy hotly.

Sighing, she nodded. "I know I did, but surely you see it's best for everyone this way."

"Best?" William scoffed. "How would *you* know what was best for anyone?"

"I'd watch my mouth if I were you, Penno," Paul said warningly. "Whether or not you are allowed any other part in our lives will strictly be up to Cassidy. Now get out before I rearrange your face with my knuckles."

William threw one last look of disgust at his sister and stomped away, no doubt feeling very ill used. "Poor William," Cassidy whispered. "He really doesn't have any clue."

Paul's hands tightened on her shoulders. He sucked in a deep breath and blew it out through his nose. "It's over. It's finally over."

She carefully stepped away from his touch and turned to face him. "Is it? Is it over for us, Paul?"

He tilted his head. "You tell me. Did you mean what you said earlier today?"

She shook her head, squeezing her eyes shut. "No. It was lies, all lies. I wanted to be as brave and selfless for you as you had been for me."

He put a hand to the back of his neck, bowed his head and looked up at her from beneath the crag of his brows. "You didn't spend the night with Tony?"

"No. Well, yes. I mean, I was afraid to go home, afraid you'd show up and convince me to let you resign your position at the company, even knowing all that would cost you, so I spent the night at Tony's. I slept on his couch. Actually, I *tried* to sleep on his couch. I spent most of the night crying.''

Paul shook his head and reached out for her, hugging her close. ''I figured it was something like that, but I'll tell you true, I'm not sure that even if it had happened, that would have been enough to keep me away from you. I love you, Cassidy Penno. I think I would forgive you anything.''

She slid her hands under his arms and hooked her arms upward around his shoulders. Leaning her head back so that she could look him in the eyes she said, ''Do you really think, given the way you treasure my virginity, that I would waste it on a boy like Tony?''

A smile lifted the corners of his mouth, and he whispered huskily, ''I was so afraid you would hate me for leaving you that night.''

''No. I only loved you all the more.''

''Nothing I've ever done has been more difficult than that.''

''I know. I found out firsthand just this afternoon how very difficult it is to give up what you want most.''

''It's only possible, I think, if it's done for someone you love even more than life itself.''

That was it exactly, the most important lesson he'd taught her. Or had they learned it together? Tears filled her eyes, tears of sheer joy, and she pulled him close to bring her mouth to his. But first...

''Paul,'' she whispered, brushing her mouth across his before pulling back a fraction of an inch, ''will you marry me?''

His answer was in his kiss. She never doubted for a moment that it was a resounding yes.

Epilogue

"**N**ow this is one of my favorites," Paul said, sliding the photograph from the album sleeve and passing it to Joyce, who reached past her distended stomach and carried the photo closer to her face for study. She lay like a beached whale in the corner of his favorite sofa, propped up with paisley pillows and a silky fringed shawl that Cass had draped over one corner to "soften and sensualize the leather."

She smiled. "Oh, yes, very nice. You make a wonderful Prince Charming."

He grinned and looked to his wife. "Yes, but what about that Cinderella?"

Cassidy giggled, thinking of the shimmering, gossamery wedding gown hung with acid-free paper and netting in a specially designed plastic bag in her closet upstairs. "Theme weddings are such fun." More fun, though, was what came after. She shivered, remembering what had transpired on their wedding night when her Prince Charming had knelt at her feet and burrowed beneath her skirts to remove her acrylic "glass" slippers.

Joyce had passed the photo to Cal, who glanced at it and handed it back to Paul. He asked Cassidy, "Have you thought of adding weddings to your consulting business?"

She wrinkled her nose. "Frankly, no. I'm booked solid for the next two years as it is. Business is so good that we're selling the costume shop to Tony."

"And then we're going to pick and choose her projects very carefully," Paul added, slipping the photo back into its sleeve and glancing at Joyce pointedly. "We're planning one of those."

"You're planning a big belly?" Joyce said, feigning ignorance. As if in retaliation for her gibe, the baby kicked her so strongly that her stomach rippled. "Ow!"

Everyone laughed and gathered around to place hands on her tummy and feel the movement. With wonder in his eyes, Cal leaned down and kissed his wife tenderly, while Cass and Paul traded envious and knowing looks.

"What is it?" Joyce's mother gasped, standing in the doorway with Cass's father at her side. Alvin had dressed up for the occasion, wearing a red-white-and-blue bandanna tied around his head and a red T-shirt with his blue jeans. The American flag hand-painted on Mary's cotton jumper and the glittering fireworks surrounding it addressed the Independence Day holiday more pointedly, and everyone on the place knew that Alvin's outfit was meant to complement hers. The two had been inseparable almost since the wedding, and the fact that they were exact opposites seemed to add to rather than detract from the attraction.

"It's nothing, Mother," Joyce called, rolling her eyes but only so her immediate companions could see.

"You're certain you're not in labor?"

"It's just the baby moving."

Mary wrung her hands. "Oh, I don't know what to think! You were born the very day you were due."

"Now, now," Alvin Penno crooned, patting Mary's shoul-

der. "William was a late baby, you know, ten days. He turned
out just fine."

A snort announced Anna Penno's presence. She pushed past
her ex-husband, crowding Mary right into his arms. Alvin
smiled down at the small woman, waggling an eyebrow las-
civiously and not caring a whit who saw it. Mary's face
blushed a becoming rose, but she didn't move away.

"What would you know about it?" Anna demanded im-
periously. "Joyce's environment is obviously hindering the
birth. She needs her lodgings purified and someone to keep
away evil humors." She glared at Alvin, implying just which
"evil humor" she had in mind.

Cassidy cringed and mouthed an apology at Joyce, who
chuckled and shook her head before calling out, "Really,
Anna? How interesting. Why don't you come and tell me all
about it?"

Cassidy could have kissed her, and she hoped that her smile
showed it. Everyone was so good to her, so understanding.
Paul's family had saved them, kept them from losing each
other. No wonder he was so devoted to them. They were all
such sweethearts, Joyce especially.

Carl and Jewel came in through the patio doors, wet from
the swimming pool, matching cover-ups belted at their waists.
"Your pool is wonderful!" Jewel gushed, toweling her hair.
"So much larger and cooler than ours."

"I've worked up quite an appetite out there," Carl said,
patting his lean middle.

Paul started to rise, laughing. "All right, all right, time to
fire up the grill."

"Ah, you sit down, son!" Alvin said, hurrying across the
room, Mary in tow at the end of his arm. "Let an old pro
handle it."

Paul subsided, but Cassidy sent him a look of alarm. Carl
intercepted it and got to his feet, murmuring, "Think I'll lend
a hand. Those new gas jets can be tricky." Cassidy breathed

a sigh of relief. As he went past her, Cal leaned down and whispered, "Better than your mother's purification rites."

Cassidy giggled again, wishing she could escape so easily as Anna settled herself in Cal's place and began to wax philosophical on Zen or some such thing. Fortunately Carl and Jewel provided an out. Laying a hand on her arm, Jewel bent close and said softly, "Darling, might we have a private word with you and Paul?"

Paul and Cassidy traded looks, then Cassidy nodded and got up. Paul led the way into the study and offered his uncle and aunt seats while Cassidy opened blinds to let sunshine into the room. Jewel refused with a smile. "Oh, no, dear, not in wet bathing suits. This won't take long, anyway. We just wanted to get your read on something."

Paul settled on the corner of the desk, and Cassidy moved to stand next to him. He wrapped an arm around her waist. "What's up?"

Jewel looked to her husband, stepped close and slipped her hand into his. Carl cleared his throat. "Well, the thing is, William came to see us the other evening."

"My William?" Cassidy asked.

Carl nodded. "You know, of course, that he and Betina have been...well, seeing one another."

"Betina's been leading him a merry chase, you mean," Paul said lightly. "What of it?"

Jewel grew distinctly uncomfortable, looking down at her sandaled feet. Carl seemed to fortify himself. "The thing is, you see, William asked for our blessing. He intends to ask Betina to marry him, and he felt that the two of you should be forewarned. He says to tell you, as well, that he'd understand if you have objections."

Cassidy rolled her eyes. William and Betina had teamed up as business partners after Paul had arranged to buy Betina's shares of the bakeries. Since then they'd enjoyed surprising success in the real estate market. It was just like William, though, to kiss up to the family before proposing. He always tried to cover his bets. Paul took the news with more aplomb— or less concern. Shrugging, he merely said, "It's nothing to me."

Jewel relaxed somewhat. "Well, of course not. We merely thought, with the family connections..."

Paul looked at Cass. "What do you think, honey? Could you bear for my stepcousin and your brother to join forces?"

"Haven't they already?"

"Looks that way to me."

"If they can stand it, I suppose we can."

"My attitude exactly," Carl said.

"Oh, I don't know," Jewel put in. "They seem fairly well suited to me."

Cassidy folded her arms, smiling wryly. "You could say that."

"Well, then," Carl said, "we're agreed." He began rubbing his hands together. "Now, " he said to his wife, "let's see how those steaks are coming along. I could eat my weight, I believe."

Jewel laughed and shook her head. "Men."

Cassidy and Paul followed them from the library, when the older couple slipped out the French doors to the patio, Paul said to his wife, "Frankly, I think they deserve each other."

A quiet moment finally came about half past nine that evening when, with the house empty, Paul and Cass went through the ground floor turning off lights and locking doors. Arm in arm, they climbed the sweeping staircase to the broad landing that overlooked the entry. There they paused and moved together, arms lightly encircling, mouths meeting gently.

"Umm." Paul lifted his head and smiled down at her. "And which room have you prepared for us tonight?"

She smiled secretively. "Ours. I thought it would be nice to utilize the balcony."

His eyes gleamed. "Oh, did you? Care to give me a hint?"

She shook her head. "You'll see."

Together they turned and moved along the landing to what was, officially, their room, not that they were any more likely to sleep there than in any of the other bedrooms in the house. Cassidy opened the door and stepped back. Paul grinned and stepped inside, right into a room that would have made the most demanding of Turkish pasha's proud. Colorful silks draped the walls and bed, creating a tentlike effect. Tasseled pillows were piled extravagantly. Persian rugs carpeted the floor. Incense burned in a brass stand. Bells tinkled lazily. Hands on his hips, Paul slowly turned in a circle to take it all in. "Amazing," he finally said.

Cassidy came in and closed the door. "Not very theme appropriate for the Fourth of July," she said, "but I wanted to surprise you."

Paul hugged her. "Thank you, sweetheart. Now get ready for bed. I just might have a surprise or two cooked up myself."

She raised an eyebrow at that. "Taking leaves from my book, Mr. Spencer?"

"Definitely, Mrs. Spencer. Now move."

Laughing, Cassidy hurried into the large, well-appointed bath and began changing into her costume. Minutes later she slipped to the door that led to the bedroom and peeked out. Paul was sitting on the foot of the bed, cross-legged. He wore only a pair of blousy, black silk pants and looked utterly delicious. Cassidy pressed a button on the intercom system that piped music into the room. As the lilting exotic notes filled the air, she lifted her veil into place and twirled into the room, the coins on her headdress and belt jangling. Paul leaned back on his elbows and enjoyed the show, laughing as she undulated provocatively just out of reach.

Finally he leaped up and caught her against him, whispering, "I always wanted my own harem. I just didn't realize that

I could have it in one woman." He plucked her veil away and kissed her before sweeping her up into his arms.

Their destination was not the bed, however, though that would come soon enough. Instead, he carried her out onto the balcony, where he lowered her bare feet to the carpet she had spread there and turned her to face the backyard. He pointed to a spot just above the tops of the trees. "Right there," he said. "Watch."

Cassidy leaned back against his chest and wrapped his arms around her bare middle, swaying to the music that wafted upon the heavy summer air. Seconds ticked by. Suddenly the dark sky erupted with colored, sparkling lights. "Fireworks! How beautiful!"

"To get a better view we'd have to be on top of the Ferris wheel at Fair Park," Paul told her.

After several minutes of breathtaking displays, Paul put his mouth next to her ear and whispered, "Now."

Missiles whistled in the distance. Pink and gold sparks flew in all directions, settling themselves into a picture of... "Cinderella!" she gasped.

Paul laughed. "It seemed appropriate. And now for the grand finale."

Red, white and blue lit up the sky with the words, "Barclay Bakeries #1 in U.S.A."

Cassidy screamed and spun around, hurling herself against her husband's bare chest. "Is it true? Really? How wonderful, Paul! I knew you could do it!"

Paul closed his arms around her and whirled her through the open doorway into the bedroom. "I wanted to break the news in a spectacular way."

"Spectacular means for spectacular news!" she gushed.

"Deserves a spectacular celebration!" Paul added.

The look in his eye left Cassidy in no doubt that it would be a very private celebration—and all the more spectacular for it.

* * * * *

Take 2 bestselling love stories FREE

Plus get a FREE surprise gift!

Special Limited-Time Offer

Mail to Silhouette Reader Service™

3010 Walden Avenue
P.O. Box 1867
Buffalo, N.Y. 14240-1867

YES! Please send me 2 free Silhouette Romance™ novels and my free surprise gift. Then send me 6 brand-new novels every month, which I will receive months before they appear in bookstores. Bill me at the low price of $2.90 each plus 25¢ delivery and applicable sales tax, if any.* That's the complete price, and a saving of over 10% off the cover prices—quite a bargain! I understand that accepting the books and gift places me under no obligation ever to buy any books. I can always return a shipment and cancel at any time. Even if I never buy another book from Silhouette, the 2 free books and the surprise gift are mine to keep forever.

215 SEN CH7S

Name	(PLEASE PRINT)	
Address	Apt. No.	
City	State	Zip

This offer is limited to one order per household and not valid to present Silhouette Romance™ subscribers. *Terms and prices are subject to change without notice. Sales tax applicable in N.Y.

USROM-98   ©1990 Harlequin Enterprises Limited

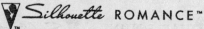

MEN at WORK

All work and no play?
Not these men!

October 1998
SOUND OF SUMMER by Annette Broadrick

Secret agent Adam Conroy's seductive gaze
could hypnotize a woman's heart. But it was
Selena Stanford's body that needed saving—
when she stumbled into the middle of an
espionage ring and forced Adam out of
hiding....

November 1998
GLASS HOUSES by Anne Stuart

Billionaire Michael Dubrovnik never lost a
negotiation—until Laura de Kelsey Winston
changed the boardroom rules. He might
acquire her business...but a kiss would cost
him his heart....

December 1998
FIT TO BE TIED by Joan Johnston

Matthew Benson had a way with words
and women—but he refused to be tied
down. Could Jennifer Smith get him to
retract his scathing review of her art by
trying another tactic: tying him *up?*

Available at your favorite retail outlet!

MEN AT WORK™

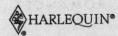 

Look us up on-line at: http://www.romance.net

PMAW3

For a limited time, Harlequin and Silhouette have an offer you just can't refuse.

In November and December 1998:

BUY **ANY** TWO HARLEQUIN
OR SILHOUETTE BOOKS and
SAVE $10.00
off future purchases

OR BUY ANY THREE HARLEQUIN OR SILHOUETTE BOOKS
AND **SAVE $20.00** OFF FUTURE PURCHASES!

(each coupon is good for $1.00 off the purchase of two
Harlequin or Silhouette books)

I accept your offer! Please send me a coupon booklet(s), to:

NAME: _____

ADDRESS: _____

CITY: _____ STATE/PROV.: _____ POSTAL/ZIP CODE: _____

Send your name and address, along with your cash register
receipts for proofs of purchase, to:

In the U.S.	In Canada
Harlequin Books	Harlequin Books
P.O. Box 9057	P.O. Box 622
Buffalo, NY	Fort Erie, Ontario
14269	L2A 5X3

PHQ4982

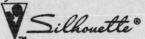

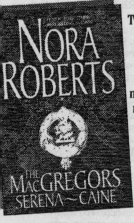

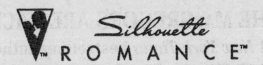

Silhouette ROMANCE™

COMING NEXT MONTH

#1336 A KISS, A KID AND A MISTLETOE BRIDE —Lindsay Longford
Virgin Brides

They had shared one magical kiss, and it had seared Gabrielle O'Shea's soul forever. Now Joe Carpenter was back—with a six-year-old son in tow. Joe didn't believe he deserved Gabby in his life again, no matter how much he—and his son—wanted her. But some loves weren't meant to be denied....

#1337 BURKE'S CHRISTMAS SURPRISE—Sandra Steffen
Bachelor Gulch/Bundles of Joy

Burke Kincaid had returned to town with a mission—to win back his lost love, Miss Louetta Graham. And when Burke found out the lovely Louetta was on her way to the altar with another man, he vowed he'd do whatever it took to be the groom at the end of the aisle.

#1338 GUESS WHAT? WE'RE MARRIED!—Susan Meier
Texas Family Ties

There was something missing in her marriage, and it wasn't just Grace Wright's memory! Her husband, Nick, was hiding something. But though she couldn't remember her marriage, the emotions Nick stirred up in her weren't easily forgotten....

#1339 THE RICH GAL'S RENTED GROOM —Carolyn Zane
The Brubaker Brides

An instant family was needed—and fast! So Patsy Brubaker went out and rented herself one handsome husband and two adorable kids. But the more time Patsy spent with sexy Justin Lassiter and their two "children," the more she wanted to keep this borrowed family forever.

#1340 STRANDED WITH A TALL, DARK STRANGER —Laura Anthony

She had never wanted a man to get close to her again. But then mysterious Keegan Winslow showed up at Wren Matthews' cabin during a blizzard. Trapped, Wren didn't want to fight her attraction to Keegan...but could she trust her heart to this handsome stranger?

#1341 A BABY IN HIS STOCKING—Hayley Gardner

One passionate encounter with her soon-to-be ex-husband, Jared, had left Shea Burroughs an expectant mother. And although Jared claimed he wasn't the crib and cradle type, Shea hoped that the season of miracles could transform Jared into a Santa Claus daddy.